An attraction they can't resist…

I was an addict, too, after all.

And a single taste of Ree wasn't enough.

I craved more of her. I wanted to devour all of her.

Piece by piece. Kiss by kiss. Touch by touch.

"I'm never letting you go," she whispered against my mouth, each word punctuated by a kiss. "Never again, Dare. I promise." Her nails raked over my back, digging in with more possessiveness than I had ever seen from her before.

Ree's need was palpable—a tangible thing I could practically reach out and grasp. It hummed through her every kiss, vibrated off her lips in waves, and cascaded into my waiting mouth, filling me.

untamed

episode 3: escaped artist

victoria green & jen meyers

Text set in Garamond

ISBN 978-1514196809

escaped artist

one
Dare

"Yes!"

Thump.

"Oh, god!"

Thump-thump.

"Ohhhh godddddd!"

Thumpthumpthumpthump.

"Yes, YES, YESSSSSS!"

I looked down at my toast and winced, my appetite vanishing faster than the groupie would once Synner was through with her. From the sound of it, it was clear she thought she was auditioning for the role of his girlfriend. Did she really think that the louder she screamed the more likely it was he'd keep her? According to Dash, the guy had no interest in relationships that lasted longer than a wham-bam-no-fucking-way, ma'am.

"You know, Dash, when you warned me that crashing with the band would be 'fucking noisy,' I was imagining drum beats and guitar riffs."

My brother looked up from his scrambled eggs and smirked. "We're recording an album called *Nailed to the Wall*. What the hell did you expect?"

"Not Synner's groupie on lead vocals." I looked toward the drummer's room—at least the door was closed this time. "That being said, I'm grateful for a place to stay. Even if it often resembles a cross between a modeling agency and a brothel."

No Man's Land was taking a break from their European tour, and in the three weeks I'd spent living with them I'd been privy to way too many tits and way too much ass. *Yes*—surprisingly, there was such a thing as an excess of T&A.

Dash laughed and ran a hand through his messy, dark hair. "You know the saying: *When in Amsterdam…*"

"*…DO all the Romans?*"

"Exactly," he said with another deep laugh. "Not to mention, you're rooming with four guys and a girl in their twenties—all of whom have very healthy…*appetites*. It's just a fact of life." As if to illustrate his point, the thumping and humping grew louder, punctuated by a couple of loud spanks. "I don't understand why you refuse to feast, Dare. You can have any woman you want. And if you ever plan on shedding that Ree chick, you're gonna have to shed your clothes with someone else."

Dash's bedroom door opened and a tall, gorgeous blonde walked out. She caught sight of Dash, and with her long hair swinging and narrow hips swaying, she catwalked over to the counter. Her lips latched on to his as her nails raked over his back in an overly-dramatic goodbye kiss.

Groaning, I looked away, my chest constricting with thoughts of Ree. Three weeks. Three fucking weeks since the gallery show. Since that prick Archer showed up with a diamond ring the size of a fucking boulder.

Jesus. Why did Dash have to bring her up? How did he know about her anyway? I hadn't said anything. Hell, I was doing everything I could to not think about her at all—the last thing I would do was actually TALK about her.

Besides, Dash and I didn't talk. Not really. We shared drinks and laughs, but we never got personal. Getting personal would mean sharing shit about our mothers, and both his and mine were way more messed up than either of us wanted to admit. It would also bring front and center the hell our asshole father had put the two families through…yeah, that was another topic I steered clear of.

"So," the blonde said, running a finger along

Dash's jaw. "Will I see you again tonight?"

Dash sighed, this regretful expression on his face. "Sorry, babe," he said. "I've got to focus on my music." She pouted, and he gently lifted her chin. "But you, and the memory of last night, will be my muse."

She looked embarrassedly pleased as he released her and waved her toward the door. He nodded at her retreating hot ass and raised a wicked eyebrow at me as if to say, *Get yourself some of that.*

But I wasn't the least bit interested.

"How many of them actually fall for that shit you just spouted?"

Dash grinned. "Every single one. Hook. Line. And sinker." Peeling his eyes away from the girl, he turned back to me. "So, you want one of your own?"

"NO." Not with Ree on my mind. "And how the hell do you know about *Ree?*"

He shrugged. "I talked to Dalia. Or, rather, Dalia talked AT me. A lot. And very loudly." Taking a deep breath, he put down his fork and aimed his dark blue gaze at me. "Look, if you want to talk—"

"I have nothing to say." Ree and I went from being two broken people who soothed each other's demons to something more. Much more. And the thought of it almost brought me to my knees. I could still see her smile every time I closed my eyes, feel her skin on my fingers, smell the ghost of her scent lingering around me, haunting me. She smelled like no one else—like honey and summer, so fucking sweet.

Shit. I shook my head, trying to force her out of my thoughts. Again.

She couldn't be mine as long as she was owned by her family. And they were never going to release her—that was clear. I was out. For real, this time.

My brother's jaw tightened as he regarded me for a moment. "You know, you're not the only person in the world who's had to let someone important go," he said quietly. "Doing the right thing is hard as hell. But doing the right thing is *right*."

"Doing the right thing is right? How enlightening. Do I smell a new hit single?"

"Fuck off, Dare. I'm just trying to help."

I rubbed at the crease that had formed between my eyebrows. "I know," I said. "I'm sorry." Dash *was* trying. I had to give him that. He'd been trying for four years now. Money when we were desperate for it. His house in Los Angeles when we'd had to flee New York. "I just don't think getting laid is going to solve my problems this time around." I shook my head. "I've already tried to fuck this girl out of my head. Trust me. And it didn't work."

"She's under your skin," he said with a nod. "You haven't painted since you got here, and Dalia said it's rare for you to go a single day without touching a brush."

Clearly, Dalia and Dash had been talking way too much.

"I'm taking a sabbatical from work right now," I said with a shrug.

"Work? Painting naked chicks is hardly work."

I tipped my head, unable to stop the small smile at his jab. "And fucking groupies is?"

"Touché." He shot me his trademark crooked smirk. The one that—according to Dalia—had made him one of rock music's most eligible bachelors. "Look at us. Living the good life." His grin soured as sarcasm laced his words. "Dad would be so proud."

I refused to talk about that bastard. Even with blood. "Look, I'm busy with the tattoo shop for the time being. No time to paint." When he'd heard I needed to get out of Paris, Rex had sent me to his former lover, Jasmine, who owned a parlor in the red-light district. As soon as she'd seen the designs I'd worked on in L.A., she'd hired me on the spot. "Right now I need the quick cash that comes with ink—painting doesn't pay. At least not yet."

Dash and I were splitting the cost of Dax and Dalia's trip to Europe. Usually they spent summers working and saving for school, but this opportunity to travel and visit me in Paris and Dash in Amsterdam had been too great. I wanted them to experience the world while they could. So I was paying for it. Happily, but I needed to be actually *making* money to be able to afford it.

"Can I come by the shop this week and have you start on the one here?" Dash pointed to a spot on his chest, right at his upper-left pec.

My eyebrows shot up. "You still haven't gotten it done? I sent you that sketch months ago. There are tattoo parlors all over Europe." I nodded at his arm. "And you've clearly stepped in one recently since that partial sleeve is new."

He pressed his lips together and looked down at his plate. "I was waiting for you to ink this one."

"Me? Why?"

"You're a brilliant artist, Dare," he said." I knew it ever since you did my first tat at that shop on Sunset."

I studied him. His jaw was tight, the expression in his eyes hard and unreadable. There was more to this than my supposed brilliance. I'd bet money on it. "This one's important to you." The design he'd asked for had been a little wren with a music note in its beak. Really different from the rest of the ink on his body. Almost…sorrowful. "You gonna tell me what it's for?"

"Just as soon as you tell me about Ree."

"Touché." I shook my head and picked up my plate. "I don't start work until two today. Why don't we head over to the shop now?"

"No way!" Indie burst into the kitchen, glaring at me. "He's not going anywhere. We have to be at the studio in fifteen minutes." She strutted over to Synner's door and pounded on it, her small frame belying her strength. "You have five seconds to get the fuck out here. Knowing you, that's more than enough time to leave a lady unsatisfied!" Then she hit the bathroom next. "Hawke!" she called out as she banged on the dark wood. "No respectable man should take such long showers unless there is a woman in there with him."

"There is," Dash said with a laugh. "*Two*, actually."

Indie groaned and shook her head of wild, insanely blue hair. "Hurry the fuck up. All of you! We gotta go!" As the lead singer and only woman in No Man's Land, Indigo Zane had quite a set of lungs on her. When she yelled, the rest of the band jumped. "Where the hell is Leo?"

"I'm almost afraid to say," Dash mumbled through a mouthful of food.

She descended on him, smacking him in the shoulder. "Spill."

"Christ, Indie. Save it for the studio." He groaned and rubbed his shoulder. "Leo went jogging."

Indie's bright blue eyes widened. "*Jogging?* NOW?"

The front door opened and Leo strode in, stopping short when he noticed Indie coming at him. "Where's the fire?" His dark skin glistened with sweat as he looked down at her fisted hands.

She got right in his face and glared up at him. "You were seriously JOGGING right now? What the hell, Leo?"

"It's *Lynx*. How many times do I have to tell you that? Fucking call me Lynx." He took a swig of his water and ran a hand over his buzzed, dark hair. "What's the problem?"

"The PROBLEM is that we'll be late to the studio. AGAIN. I swear it's like I'm babysitting four fucking toddlers. EVERYONE," she yelled, hands on her hips, blue hair swinging. The thumping stopped suddenly and the shower turned off. "Get your asses out here! NOW! This album isn't going to record itself!"

I downed the rest of my coffee and backed out of the room with raised hands, heading for the door. "That's my cue. I've seen both Synner's and

Hawke's bare asses way too many times already. I'm out."

I shut the door behind me, escaping the chaos, shaking my head at the insanity that was Dash's life. I had no idea how he did it.

But, truth be told, his chaos was kind of welcomed.

It kept thoughts of Ree out of my head.

two
Reagan

People swarmed the cobblestone streets around me as I walked all alone in a city of strangers. At least Dare was here. Somewhere. I hadn't seen him yet, but I knew his brother's band was in town. Thankfully, Dalia had taken pity on me and given me their address.

"I'm sorry, Ree," she'd said when she answered his door back in Paris. "He left." She'd stepped out into the hall and closed the door behind her.

"Left?" I'd said, my knees feeling weak. "How could he already be gone?"

She bit down on her lip, her beautiful features tinged with sadness. "I'm sorry…"

"No," I said. "You have nothing to apologize for. It's my fault. I'm the one who's sorry. And I shouldn't be putting you in this position but…" I searched her face. "Would you…can you tell me where he is? *Please?*"

"He asked me not to." Her teeth sank farther into her lip as her eyebrows tilted toward each other. "More like *ordered* me not to."

My eyes started to water and I furiously blinked back tears as I fought to keep my breathing under control. "I understand," I choked out. There were other ways to find him, of course. It wasn't like I hadn't picked up *any* tricks from my parents, but I had so hoped she'd tell me. "Okay. Thanks, Dal." I took a step back, but Dalia reached out to stop me, her hand light on my arm. My gaze lifted to meet hers.

"Ree…do you love him?" She peered intensely into my eyes.

My head was nodding before she finished, my words coming out in a tight whisper. "With all that I am and everything that I have."

"*Well…*" Her eyes narrowed as she studied me. "It's not like I ever do what he says anyway. He's in Amsterdam with Dash. And he's being a complete idiot, if you ask me."

A laugh sputtered up and out of my mouth even as the tears overflowed. I half-laughed, half-sobbed as Dalia hugged me.

"He needs you," she said into my hair, which only made me cry harder. "And he loves you, too. I don't think my brother has ever loved someone. Not like this. Not like you."

She released me and I reached up to wipe off my face. "Thank you," I said quietly. "Thank you, thank you, THANK YOU."

She nodded with a grin. "Just...don't hurt him. He's a stubborn son-of-a-bitch, but he's my favorite brother."

The apartment door flew open and Dax stood there glaring at Dalia. "*WHAT DID YOU JUST SAY?!*"

"Oh, don't get your frilly panties in a twist, Dax," she said. "I knew you were there the whole time—stop eavesdropping on us already." She rolled her eyes, turning to me again. "I meant that Dare is my favorite brother outside of Dax." He folded his arms across his chest and leaned against the doorframe with a satisfied smirk as she said, "And you need to be good to him because I really don't wanna have to hunt you down if you break his heart."

Another laugh bubbled up within my chest. God, I loved her. "I won't. His heart is safe with me. I swear."

Dax lifted an eyebrow at me and winked. "You can come break my heart anytime you want, babe." Dalia spun around, smacked his arm, and shoved him back into the apartment as his deep laughter echoed out into the hall.

Even now, as I walked along the canal, the city

lit up, amber lights shining like fire on the water as blue hues filled the spaces in between, I couldn't help but smile at the thought of Dalia and Dax. They'd stayed in Paris for a week before catching a train to Rome. And they'd be coming to Amsterdam later this summer to see No Man's Land in concert. I only hoped I'd still be here by then. And that things would be good.

Sabine had understood when I'd called to tell her I was leaving La Période Bleue and didn't know when I'd be back.

"*Pour l'amour? Bien sûr.*" *For love? Of course.* "You MUST go, *chérie.* You must say *oui à l'amour.* This Wilde…he is your great love. I knew that from the first time I met him."

She had contacts in Amsterdam and had set me up with a couple of interviews at some local galleries. I had no idea whether I'd be able to find work here, but at least I had a little bit of money to keep me going for a while. The work I'd done in Paris made a huge difference, and Sabine still insisted on sticking to our terms and paying me for Marie Ormonde's show even though I'd left before it opened.

I owed her big.

She was making it possible for me to have the life I wanted.

To reinvent myself.

I reached into my bag, my fingers closing around the familiar folded-up piece of paper. My phoenix—what had become my source of strength and inspiration over the years. The one item in my purse I reached for first, instead of pills.

Well, *most* of the time.

I wasn't perfect. And some old habits were hard to break. Especially at night. In the dark. When I was all alone.

I'd be lying if I said I hadn't numbed the shit out of myself those first few days without Dare.

Again.

But I was trying. Even if I had slipped just this afternoon before I'd stepped out of my apartment. Needles scared the crap out of me—I needed a little pharmaceutical courage if I was going to go through with this.

Because before I sought out Dare, I wanted to have his bird—*my* bird—imprinted on my body in ink. Maybe its strength would infuse itself into my skin, into my mind, into my soul.

If I had his art on my body when I came to apologize, he'd know. He'd know how much I loved him. It would have to mean something to him. It sure as hell meant EVERYTHING to me. Enough that I was willing to brave needles.

Nothing would stop me this time. Not my

parents. Not the nightmares. Not even Dare.

I needed this bird, and then I needed to find him. To explain. I needed him to understand.

Fuck, I needed *him*.

Breaking free wasn't something that could be done in one fell swoop. At least not with my family. My parents weren't used to losing. In their minds, my freedom was their loss. Their failure. *Fail is not in my vocabulary,* my father had said. He wasn't kidding. He didn't take failure well. AT ALL. And me not going to Harvard and refusing to follow the path they'd meticulously marked out for me reeked of failure to him.

I knew this, and I knew that getting out from under him would be akin to a twelve-step program. Dare didn't understand this about my family. But from everything that had happened in Paris, and all that Dalia had told me, at least I knew he loved me.

That tiny piece of knowledge was enough to keep me going. I wasn't going to give up that easily.

The issue now was finding the right tattoo shop. There had to be a hundred of them in Amsterdam, and I'd already visited dozens today, but none of them caught my eye. Somehow, I felt like the work of the parlor had to affect me like a great piece of art—when I came across the one that did, I'd know it was the right place for me and my phoenix.

So I braved the fear and the pain in my feet, and kept going. Even though it was late. Even though I'd been looking all day long already, was exhausted and ready to crash. The beauty of this majestic place, with its grand architecture and old city feel, should have been enough to entice me to keep moving, exploring, searching, yet there was something stronger that spurred me on.

Dare. Always Dare. Just one more, for Dare.

And so I turned another street corner with windows full of beautiful girls glowing crimson in the dark of night. Ahead on the right, I spotted yet another tattoo parlor—black front with gold lettering, a bright red sign lighting up the window. As I got closer, I could see the name of it clearly.

Vogel Tattoos.

The name brought me to a full stop. Vogel? Like Rex Vogel? That had to be some kind of a sign. Chills tumbled down my spine as I took a few slow steps toward the shop, my eyes scouring the art.

Magnificent birds in all styles graced the display in the window, along with animals, symbols, and words written in beautiful scripts. If I didn't already have the perfect design clutched in my hand, I would be hard pressed to pick from the samples in front of me. Not to mention, I was certain they had even better designs by the hundreds inside.

This was the place. Without a doubt. A strange calm settled over my mind as excitement shot through my heart, kicking my pulse up. I grinned at my reflection in the shop window. I was seconds away from getting my phoenix and becoming reborn.

New Ree. New me. I was starting now.

More sure of the step I was about to take than of anything else I'd done in my life, I opened the door to the shop, ready to claim my freedom.

three
Dare

"Keep the bandage on until at least noon tomorrow," I said to the blonde splayed across my table. "Resist the temptation to show it off until then."

She raised an eyebrow at me, hopped off the table, and peeled back the wrapping, wiggling her butt in her twin's face. "Hot or what?"

"So hot, Izzy." Her sister smacked her ass as I tried to hide my irritated groan.

Izzy fixed her dark brown eyes on me, lifting her shirt up much farther than it needed to go. "And what do you think?"

The tiny butterfly on her lower back won zero creativity points with me, but she was a paying client. And the client was always right. "It's great. Just don't touch it or it could get infected."

"God, I wasn't talking about the tattoo," she said with a giggle. "So...you also do piercings, right?"

"Yeah, we do."

"Everywhere?"

I nodded. "What would you like done?"

"I'm not sure..." Her high heels clacked against the hardwood floor as she strutted over to me. She placed a hand on my chest and tilted her head up, an unmistakable expression in her hooded gaze. "What's the most intimate place you've ever pierced a girl?"

"We have a great female technician who would be happy to pierce anything you want as long as you can withstand the pain," I said. "Want me to get her in here?"

Izzy's bravado melted a little, and I couldn't help but grin. The threat of an actual piercing always deflated posers like her. She pulled her hand away and tugged down her shirt.

"Umm...maybe another time." Glancing over at her sister, she said, "We're going to Jimmy Woo. Apparently there is a celeb-studded VIP event there tonight. Do you want to come?"

She was the third chick to ask me out today. The later in the day it got, the more buzzed they were, and the quicker the invitations came. Especially around midnight.

I shook my head. "Can't. We're open until three." She didn't have to know that she was my last appointment and I was off in ten minutes.

"Wow. That late?" She stuck out her lip. "Or, rather, so early?"

I shrugged. "The best business hours in the red-light district happen once the sun goes down and the lights come on."

"What about meeting us back at our place?" Izzy's sister said. "We have a room at The Toren." She took her sweet time dragging a bright pink wand over her already glossy lips. "ONE room. As twins, we've gotten used to sharing our playthings." Then she winked.

Way to be subtle.

"Thanks for the offer, but I'll have to pass. I'm really swamped tonight." And so not interested.

"Too bad," the girl said, then turned to her sister with a haughty grin. "God, Daddy would've killed us if he heard that we hooked up with a tattoo artist. He's already going to freak when he finds out we got these matching butterflies."

"Happy to save him the double homicide charge." I guided them out of the room. "Thanks for stopping by, ladies."

"If you change your mind, we're in the penthouse suite!" Izzy shouted over her shoulder.

Rich and looking for trouble, the two of them reminded me of the girl I was trying so damn hard to forget. But even though Ree had been so different when I first met her—privileged, afraid to live, broken—there had always been something real about her. Something true. Something these girls couldn't even dream of possessing.

Sia walked into the room, eyeing the pair on their way out. "I've got another girl for you if you're willing to hang around for a bit longer. Good money for this one."

I groaned. "Let me guess, another stoned college student looking to rebel by getting a flowery tattoo? You promised you'd take the next chick. How about you send me a three-hundred pound biker or at least someone wanting a design that's not straight out of one of our books?"

"You underestimate me, Dare." She wagged her finger at me, shaking her long, straight, black mane of hair. "I'm bringing you something special."

"Is that so? Keep talking and I might be able to stay an extra hour or so."

"I know all about your phoenix obsession that our dear Vogel started," she said as she handed me a worn-looking piece of paper. "It's a pretty intricate design and the client is a tat virgin, so I told her she should come back tomorrow when you have more time, but she was insistent on getting started right away. I thought maybe you'd want to check it out and talk to her about the process and number of sessions it's going to take."

"Let me see this sketch. If it's going to take a few—" I glanced down at the paper as I opened it.

NO.

I could feel the blood draining out of my body.

No. *Fucking.* Way.

Sia's bright red lips were moving a mile a minute, but I couldn't hear the words coming out of her mouth.

The paper scorched my hand.

Two parts. One whole. The words—in my own fucking handwriting—burned into my vision under a familiar phoenix that blazed across the page.

My phoenix. No. Not mine. *Ree's.*

"Where is she?" My voice was hoarse, sounded like it came from someone else.

Sia gaped at me. "Where is who, hun?"

I pushed past her, and strode out into the front parlor. A part of me hoped it was all a misunderstanding. That someone had somehow gotten their hands on my sketch. That was it. I would just say this phoenix didn't belong to them and steer them to another design.

This bird didn't belong to anyone anymore. The girl who used to own it had given up. Way too fucking easily.

But there was a tiny, insane, addicted piece of me that wanted it to be Ree.

It was that part I feared most.

The moment my eyes connected with a pair of stormy blue ones, my heart lodged in my throat. There was something sickening about having your greatest hope and worst fear confirmed at the same time. In the same person.

"Dare…" Ree breathed, my name barely a whisper on her lips. God, those lips. Those fucking kissable lips.

Get a grip, man. Get her out of your head.

"What the hell are you doing here?" I didn't mean to sound so severe, but the words just shot out of my mouth, sharp as daggers.

A war waged inside me, a battle between my heart and mind. The wounded, irrational part of me wanted to scoop her up, crush her against me, and never let her go. But I knew I had to hold back or risk a repeat of New York and Paris. I had no intention of getting into WWIII with her family. Not after everything I'd overheard between her and that preppy, blond douchebag. Not when she wouldn't fight for us.

"I don't understand…" She looked around the shop, her gaze brimming with genuine confusion and surprise. "You work here? You tattoo?"

"Some of us have to work for a living, Princess. Unlike your fiancé, my dad didn't leave me a cushy trust fund to fall back on."

Hurt filled her eyes, and I immediately regretted my words. Fuck. No one but Ree was capable of making me lose my composure and spin out of control like this.

"He's not my fiancé," she whispered, taking a step toward me. "And I...I just didn't know you did this."

That sweet scent that was so very her wafted over me. It wasn't something that came out of an expensive bottle, nor found anywhere else. It was just her. Pure Ree. Pure intoxication. One whiff and I couldn't remember my name. My own personal drug of choice.

But, damn it all to hell, I was quitting her cold turkey.

I shrugged like I didn't care that she was standing right in front of me, looking up at me with those big, watery eyes as if I was the answer to her prayers. What was that saying? Fake it till you make it? I was drowning in fake, getting suffocated by my pretend indifference.

"There are a lot of things you don't know about me," I said.

That thought hit me hard. There were still so many things we didn't know about each other, secrets she refused to talk about. Shit that was no longer my business. No matter how much I wanted it to be.

Fuck. Focus. "What are you doing here?"

"I…" Her bottom lip quivered, and I stuffed my hands into my pockets to keep myself from reaching out to touch it. "I'm here to get a tattoo," she said. "I saw the name of the shop and had to come in."

I shook my head, waving the piece of paper in my hand. "I'm not going to ink this on you."

She crossed her arms over her chest. "Why not?"

"Because it doesn't belong to you."

Her eyes narrowed and her face flushed red. "Yes, it does. It's *my* phoenix."

"Not anymore, Reagan." It physically hurt to call her by that name, but I had to keep reminding myself she was no longer my Ree.

She stared at me, her mouth gaping, steam practically coming out her ears as she geared up to ream me out.

At that moment, Sia walked up behind me and placed a hand on my elbow. "Do you two know each other?" she asked, sizing Ree up.

Ree's eyes widened, her gaze falling to Sia's hand, then quickly shooting back up to her face. Her head tilted to one side. "You—"

"I'm Sia," she said, sliding her hand along my arm. Claiming me.

And fuck it all, I let her do it even though her touch was the last thing I wanted. Just to see the look on Ree's face. Her eyes stayed glued to Sia's fingers as they brushed my arm, pain eclipsing all other emotions in them. I knew that pain vividly, having felt the full force of it three weeks ago in my own fucking stairwell when I watched that pompous ass get down on one knee.

After a moment, Ree snapped out of it. "Sia?" Recognition flooded her face. "Dare painted you."

Sia laughed. "I guess you DO know each other. Yes, I was his *first* nude." She practically purred the words as she added, "We spent a lot of time *sans* clothing that summer. And I sculpted some very *intimate* pieces of him."

"Oh." Ree swallowed hard. Shit. It was too much. I'd let it go too far. I shook off Sia's hand and shot her a look that I hoped to god she would understand as a very stern *back off.*

Yeah, I was being an ass and hurting Ree. Still, that didn't mean I'd let anyone else do it. A fucking double standard, but what of it? She'd hurt me and payback was a bitch, but there was a limit to how far I would go.

"Well, it's nice to meet a friend of Dare's," Ree

said, glancing up at my face. There was a question floating in the depths of her eyes, but she seemed unable to ask it.

She looked so...lost. Which fucking killed me.

I shook my head, once again reminding myself she wasn't my problem anymore. "Look, I have to get back to work," I said. "I have an appointment coming in soon." Lie. "Maybe you can get your fiancé to take you to another tattoo shop. I'm sure he can afford to buy you whatever you want, Princess. Hell, he could even buy you your own fucking parlor." I turned and began walking toward the back room.

Ree followed me inside, slipping through the curtain before I had a chance to do anything about it. "Stop it, Dare. Stop acting like this." She grabbed my arm and pulled me around to face her. And I let her do it. Her touch felt too damn good to resist.

Jesus. She was a drug. And I was gladly gulping it down. What the fuck was wrong with me? I needed to get away from her. Far, far away.

"This isn't you," she said. "This isn't *us*."

"It is now. You made your choice." I took a step back, giving us some distance, getting away from the heat of her body. If she only didn't smell so fucking good.

"I'm not with Archer. I never was. That was just

my parents—"

"I don't care," I said through clenched teeth.

Another lie.

She knew it. She stepped forward, pressing herself against me.

"I came to Amsterdam for you." Her chest rose and fell against mine, her breath warmed my lips.

"Why? Why the hell did you even bother?"

She stared at me, her waterblue eyes threatening to drown me. "Because I fucking love you, you ass. God, Dalia was right. You are an idiot."

Dalia *again?* Man, my baby sister really needed to learn to keep her mouth shut about me.

"I don't care." Liar, liar, *liar.* "I'm tired of being sucked into your blue-blood problems," I told her. "Pretty Boy was right. I have nothing to offer you."

"That's not true. You have everything I need. You ARE everything I need." Ree reached out to touch my face, but I stopped her by wrapping my fingers around her wrist. "I love you, Dare Wilde. That's why I'm here." She pushed against me, sending us off-balance and tumbling into the table behind me.

And that was it. Her presence enveloped me, extinguishing my resolve.

She, too, was everything, and I was completely sunk in her, in us, in *this.*

To hell with it all, I needed her. Wanted her. Craved her with all that I was.

I wove my fingers through her hair and pulled her close, breathing her in. "I'm so tired of playing games with you, Ree."

"I'm not playing." Tears filled her eyes, making them shine. "I swear, Dare. This is the real me. Please don't push me away. Let me be yours once and for all."

With each quick, short breath, she moved closer and closer, parting her lips in anticipation. All I wanted to do was to taste her, take her, make her all mine. But something stopped me cold.

Her pupils were dilated, her eyes glassy, her lids heavy.

If I didn't have so much experience with my mother and her relapses, I wouldn't have thought twice about it. Because I would've missed the signs.

Clear as fucking day. And un-*fucking*-believable.

"Are you HIGH? Right now? *Again?*" Tightening my grip on her, I fought the urge to shake her. Shake some fucking sense into her. "Do you not realize what you're doing to yourself? What the hell is wrong with you, Ree?"

She opened her mouth to say something, then closed it again. Her façade cracked. Waves of anguish flooded her eyes. A whole tsunami of them. And I was the cause of it. Shit.

"*Everything*," she finally whispered. "Everything is wrong with me!"

Then she tore away from my grip and fled the room, leaving me alone, stunned. And torn. She was a junkie—I already had one of those in my life, and one was more than enough.

But this was Ree.

Fuck.

I heard the bell jingle right before the front door banged close, and looked down to see the phoenix drawing still in my hand.

four
Reagan

Idiot. Loser. Fuck-up.

Dare hadn't said those words to me, but I'd heard them all the same. After all, it was who I was, who I'd always been my whole messed up life. I thought I had changed these past three years. I thought leaving my old life behind had meant something, that I'd come so far.

But it was all just a big fucking lie.

I was no different than before—same mistakes, same stupid decisions, same fears, same pills. Same Reagan McKinley. I simply had less money to throw around at my problems and probably one less friend. I hadn't spoken to Archer since I'd not-so-graciously turned down his proposal.

People didn't change. Seasons did, fashions and trends could, even mayors and governors. But not the people in my life. My family never would.

And obviously I couldn't either.

Dare had made that painfully clear tonight.

All I wanted to do was pop more pills. Forget everything. Stop feeling.

Case in point—my first thought was to find refuge in the pills. Even though those little bastards were to blame for this situation tonight. For once, I was grateful the bottle was back in my flat rather than in my bag. At least I still had my—

Oh, shit.

I didn't even have to search my bag to know it wasn't there. I stopped cold on the sidewalk. Someone bumped into me, muttered something in Dutch, and glared as he walked around me.

The phoenix. *My phoenix.*

I didn't have my bird. My anchor. My strength.

Oh, god.

Panic rose deep within me, shaking my soul loose, threatening to break me into thousands of tiny little pieces.

I crouched down on the ground and dumped the contents of my bag onto the cobblestones even though I knew the move was futile. My wallet *thunked* to the ground, a lip gloss rolled into a crack, keys jingled out. But no paper. No phoenix.

Dare still had it.

I couldn't breathe. If I didn't have my bird and I didn't have my pills…how was I going to survive this moment? What about the next? And all those dark nights that were undoubtedly coming? Hot tears began to roll down my face as I fought hard to keep from breaking down and sobbing.

"Hey," someone said as he knelt down next to me, "you need some help with that?"

As he reached for my lip gloss, I noticed his entire forearm was covered in colorful tattoos that wound around him like a sleeve of art. The letters P L A Y were inked onto the fingers of his right hand, and H A R D on his left. He dropped the pink vial into my bag and then did the same with my wallet and the rest of my stuff as I continued to stare at him in awe.

Intense green eyes gazed into mine questioningly and a cigarette hung off his thin lips. Then he pulled it out of his mouth, aiming a dazzling smile at me.

For some stupid reason, I started to cry again.

"Aw, it can't be that bad, can it, love?" he said in a deep voice warmed by a British accent. "Not for a beautiful girl like you."

He had no idea.

The guy stood up and I followed, feeling so lost. I didn't want to go home because I knew I'd never be able to resist the pills, and with the way I was feeling right now that whole bottle was going to look much too inviting. But I had nowhere else to go. I wasn't welcome at Vogel Tattoos—Dare probably wouldn't even talk to me now. I'd have to return and try again when I was sober. Maybe tomorrow. If I was going to have any chance with him at all, my apology couldn't be laced with chemical courage.

"Why don't you let me buy you a drink?" the Brit said, pushing his dirty blond hair out of his eyes. He smiled and reached out a hand to me. "I'm Synner, by the way."

I studied his face—he wasn't giving off any creepy vibes, thank god. He just seemed genuinely friendly and obviously interested. And right now, at this very moment, what I needed more than anything else in the world was a friend.

So I shook his outstretched hand and forced a smile. "Reagan."

The first three shots felt like firewater. But the following three, I didn't feel at all. Synner was remarkably entertaining as he spoke about his many tattoos. I pointed to a blue feather that was hidden in the intricate design on his arm.

"What about this one?" I said.

His jaw tightened and he shook his head. "Sorry, love. That one I don't talk about."

I could understand that. Everyone had their

secrets. Some more than others. And I certainly wasn't spilling any of mine tonight. Or any other night for that matter.

"I went to get a tattoo earlier," I told him, my words coming out slightly slurred. "But he wouldn't do it. He hates me."

Synner arched a pierced eyebrow. "Who hates you?"

I stared into my empty shot glass, wondering why it wasn't magically filling back up anymore. The room swayed when I turned my head to look at my new friend.

"The only man I've ever loved my whole fucking life."

"Then he's clearly daft. Who could hate a creature as sweet as you?" He wound my hair around his finger and gently tugged it toward him.

I shook my head, pulling the lock free from his grasp. "*He* does," I said with a groan. "And he should. He has every reason to."

"Why don't you," Synner said, leaning forward so our lips were nearly touching, "let *me* love you tonight? One night with me and you won't be thinking about this guy anymore. I can promise you that."

I smiled at him, then placed my hands on his chest and pushed him away.

"But I don't want you." I sighed. "I only want

him."

"Haven't you ever heard that you're supposed to love the one you're with?" He winked. "Or at least let him love you. I'll make your head spin, I promise. In many sinful ways and even more sinful positions."

I laughed then, because COME ON. "Does that line EVER work for you?" I said.

A deep, hearty laugh rose from his chest as he grinned at me. "Bloody hell. I've never had to work this hard to get some looker into my bed," he said. "You have no idea what you're missing out on. They don't call me Syn JUST because I'm hot as hell."

Synner was hot, all right. Smokin' hot. Tattoos covering his body, not an ounce of body fat, muscles giving his arms contours, but not filling him out. His dirty blond hair was tucked behind his ears, stray strands falling across his eyes. Once upon a time, I would have jumped into his bed without thinking twice.

But he wasn't my Dare.

"Sorry," I said, the laugh dying in my throat as my thoughts returned to Dare. Everything was so screwed up. I had no idea whether I'd be able to fix it. "I don't mean to mess with your flawless *shag* record."

He lifted his beer, took a swig, and tilted the

bottle at me. "S'okay. A little humility never hurt anyone." He nodded at my shot glass. "Why don't you let me help you home? You've had a lot of those."

I shook my head, the room tilting precariously as I tried to get up. But I immediately lost my balance and slid off the barstool. Synner caught me, setting me back upright.

"Nah." I waved him off. "I'm fine."

"You're anything but fine, love." He smiled at me again, his teeth straight and white.

And he was right. I was nowhere near fine. I wasn't even on the same continent as fine.

"Where are you staying?" His words floated over to me as if coming from afar.

My mind churned at an annoyingly slow pace as I tried to remember the name of my hostel. The Riding Donkey? The Laughing Cow? If I'd known this city better, I probably would have been able to find my way back, but at the moment I couldn't even remember the name of the street I was staying on.

Shit. Could this night get any worse?

"I have no idea." I mumbled the words, not even sure if I was coherent anymore. The whole bar swirled around me, and I had the vague notion that perhaps if I hadn't been too nervous to eat all day the alcohol wouldn't be hitting me quite this hard.

"Alright," Synner said as he stood up. "You can come crash at my flat. I can't, in good conscience, leave you here to fend for yourself." He leaned down, pulled one of my arms up around his neck, and wrapped his arm around my waist. Then he lifted me up so I was standing in front of him.

I started to pull away. "I'm not sleeping with you."

"I know that, love."

My brow furrowed, my thoughts colliding into one another.

"Synner?" I said. "Why are you being nice to me? You don't even know me."

He just shrugged. "I have younger sisters. And somewhere, in the center of this irresistibly hot, sex-god before you, there is an honest-to-goodness beating heart. I don't want you getting hurt."

My throat tightened, and I nodded, then walked with him toward the door. The room pitched and my stomach lurched. We'd just barely made it outside when I felt everything I'd drunk coming back up.

I ripped myself away from him and grabbed for the side of a building. Then I heaved onto the street, over and over again until I felt the world spinning and everything going black.

five
Reagan

I came to in a dark room, and if it hadn't been for the streetlight spilling in through the windows, I would have freaked the fuck out. But I wasn't in a cellar. I was above ground.

And I was okay. Well, for now.

*Oh, god...*where the hell was I?

"No fucking way, Synner." A deep voice rang out, and I lifted my pounding head to see two men silhouetted in the doorway. "Not cool at all, man. She's completely wasted. You're sleeping on the couch tonight. You step one foot in this bedroom and I'll cut your dick off."

"Bloody hell," Synner said. "Give me some fucking credit. I'm not that guy. I don't need to be."

I squinted into the darkness, trying to make out the other guy's features, which was almost impossible since he was backlit. He was taller than

Synner, had longer hair, and something about his face seemed familiar.

"It's NOT okay, Syn."

"Agreed. That's why I'm standing here talking to you and not balls deep like some degenerate git. I only do the ready and very willing." Synner crossed his arms over his chest, and leaned against the doorjamb. "What are you still doing up, anyway?"

The other man shrugged a shoulder. "Nothing."

"The girl?" Synner said.

"The girl." A deep sigh floated through the open door. "Always the girl."

"Don't say I didn't warn you." As I watched Synner shake his head, my own started to spin again. "You've gotta let it go. Losing your mind over someone you can't have will fuck you up. That's why I don't bother anymore." He clapped the other guy on the back. "Alright, that's enough chick chat for the month. You better catch some sleep while you still can. Indie's going to be screeching at us before dawn."

Their words started to fade away as exhaustion, alcohol, and drugs weighed down my body and my eyelids. The blessed oblivion of sleep swept over me, pulling me under, erasing my every thought.

A loud bang on the door jolted me awake. Someone yelled. Sweet baby Jesus, her voice was so damn shrill. The sound was like an ice pick being pounded into my brain. Over and over and over again. I pulled the pillow over my head and crushed it to my ears.

Fucking hell, who was making all that noise?

"GET UP! NOW!" she yelled. "We're going to be late again!"

Shit. If she didn't stop shrieking like a freaking banshee, my head was going to explode. Daylight streaming in from the window had been bad enough when I'd opened my eyes, but the sheer volume of her voice was splitting my head in two.

I gripped the pillow tighter, bracing for her next call.

But all that followed was silence.

Thank god.

I dragged the pillow off my head, slowly lifted it, and looked around. Christ, just moving my eyes hurt.

Where the hell was I?

The room was large and painted a deep red, clothes were strewn all over, and there a bunch of drumsticks sticking out of a vase on the dresser. I had no clue where I was or how I'd gotten here.

Or what I'd done in this bed.

Crap. My hands shot down to my chest to check for clothes. I almost cried in relief when I realized that everything was intact.

I gingerly lay my head back down, letting it sink into the pillow that felt more like a brick, and willed my brain to backtrack. *Yesterday.* What happened yesterday?

As my memory returned, I shook my head, the thoughts rattling around in my skull.

Dare. The tattoo parlor. Losing my phoenix.

Probably losing my chance with Dare.

Then I'd left and gone to a bar with some guy. Skimmer? Skipper? Something weird like that. God, I couldn't even remember his name.

And I couldn't remember anything that happened.

Oh, god…oh god, oh god…

I started shaking as the immensity of what I had done settled over me. How fucking stupid could one person really be? How could I have put myself in that position?

Jesus.

I slowly sat up, then put my throbbing head in my hands as I waited for the room to stop spinning. My stomach lurched, and I felt like I was going to be sick. From the disgusting taste in my mouth, I was pretty sure I'd already done that at least once last night.

God. I had to stop this. I just wished I knew how.

A 4.0 GPA from Columbia apparently didn't cure stupidity.

I took a few deep breaths. I was okay. Nothing had happened last night. I just needed to get my stuff together and get out of here. At least the yelling had stopped, and maybe I could just sneak out without anyone seeing me.

I pulled the covers off my body, slid my legs over the edge of the bed, and stood up slowly. God, every footstep was like a jab straight to my brain. Getting home was going to suck major ass.

It took forever and a day to reach the door. I pressed my ear against it and listened for a moment. There was the low rumble of conversation, but no more yelling. Thankfully. I opened the door as quietly as I could, hoping it wouldn't squeak, praying the way out would be obvious and easy to reach. I had no interest in wandering around some stranger's house right now.

I needed to get back to my hostel, take the longest shower of my life, and then try again with Dare. Stone-cold sober this time.

The door opened onto a living room to my

right and a kitchen on the left. Two tall guys stood around the kitchen counter with their backs to me. I only glanced at them briefly, not wanting to draw their attention, figuring one of them had to be the guy from last night. With a hangover the size of Manhattan, I wasn't sure I would even be able to recognize him. The strong, bitter smell of coffee hit, and a wave of nausea washed over me. Damn it. Why did people have to drink that nasty stuff? Especially first thing in the morning.

"GUYS!"

Oh, dear god. The yeller was back, standing about ten feet away from me. She was this petite little pixie with bright blue hair and eyes to match. I never would have guessed someone so small—and *blue*, for that matter—could make that much noise. Her voice cut through my head like a jagged knife, and I winced, grabbing my temples instinctively to prevent the pain from burrowing deeper.

"Oh, shit," she said in a much quieter, but still equally torturous, tone. "Sorry, girl." Giving me a quick inspection she added, "Damn, you look like hell."

No shit. I felt like hell.

"And you…" I opened my eyes and raised one agonizing eyebrow. "…look like a Smurf."

She smirked and nodded toward the living

room. "Door's that way. Don't let it hit you on the a—"

"*Ree?!*"

NO.

No, no, no…*please* no. It couldn't be.

My chest constricted, squeezing all the air from my lungs as my hands began to shake. I didn't want to turn around and look into those dark brown eyes.

Why couldn't I catch a break?

Why, out of all the houses in this huge fucking city, did I have to end up in this one? Out of all the people in Amsterdam, why did I have to meet Slim Jim or whatever the fuck his name was?

Because even though I was pretty damn certain nothing had happened, Dare would never believe me. Not after everything that stood between us.

Hell, I wouldn't believe me either at this point.

"Un-*fucking*-believable." His words hissed out at me, tearing through my chest, breaking my heart. I turned, lifted my eyes to meet his, then immediately wished I hadn't. Anger burned so bright in them it made me wince. Anger, hurt, and betrayal. Again.

Fuck. Me.

I shook my head, then wished I hadn't done that either. "It's not—"

"Save it," he said. Each word felt like a blade to

my head and my heart. "Don't bother, Ree. We're over, remember?" Then he turned and stalked away.

I stared after him, tears filling my eyes, unable to stop him from leaving me. Unable to speak…because there was just too much to say. Oceans of unspoken explanations, misunderstandings, and secrets separated us. Could love really be enough to overcome all this? I didn't know anymore. I was starting to believe there was no hope for us.

I watched him retreat from me, feeling like every already-broken piece of my heart was shattering even further.

"So you're Ree, huh?" A dark-haired guy leaned against the counter in the kitchen, his voice deep and soft when he spoke. He had denim blue eyes that seemed both foreign and familiar. There was something about his chiseled face that calmed me, though I couldn't for the life of me place him.

"Yeah." I nodded, the pain in my head reminding me too late that all motion was bad.

"I'm Dash," he said, and all feeling left my body. Great. What a delightful way to finally meet Dare's older brother. Good going, Reagan. He stepped toward me, a warm smile on his face that I couldn't quite comprehend. Shouldn't he be judging me, condemning me? "Let me help you find a cab. You'll probably have more luck talking to Dare later. After he's had some time to cool off."

He walked past me, opened the door, and waited. I followed, the shock of his kindness leaving me speechless. The sympathy of strangers was a funny thing. Why were they all so much nicer to me than my own family? Than Dare?

Maybe it was me. Maybe to actually *know* me was to hate me.

Not that it mattered. At this moment, no one hated me more than I hated myself.

six
Dare

I was going to kill him.

"Open up, Synner!" I pounded on the bathroom door. It was locked, but I had enough rage in me to rip it from the hinges. "Get out here! NOW!"

The sound of running water punctuated my roars. He always took his sweet time in the shower after a long night doing god-knows-what with his latest conquest.

Except this morning that conquest was Ree.

MY Ree.

Goddamn it, I was going to rip his fucking head off.

"SYNNER!"

"That dude is setting the record for Amsterdam ass." Hawke, the bass player, jabbed my shoulder as he passed me on the way out of his room. "Did you see that hot blonde he brought home last night? *Damn*. Too bad he doesn't like to share booty."

Alright then, Hawke was going to die next.

My fist formed a small crack in the wood. "Open this fucking do—"

The door swung open and Synner stood in front of me, wide-eyed, soaking wet, and naked.

"Bloody hell! Who jizzed in your coffee this morning?" He pulled a towel off the rack and wrapped it around his waist. "What the hell is the matter with you?"

"What the hell is the matter with ME?" I saw red. My chest heaved, my fury spurred on by his blasé attitude. Could he care any less about the girl he'd just fucked? "What the hell is the matter with YOU, asshole? Out of all the women in Amsterdam your STD-ridden dick could've harassed last night, you had to pick mine?"

Synner's eyebrow shot up. "STD-ridden? Harassed? That hurts." He put a hand to his ink-covered heart, then looked me right in the eye. "And, for your information, my incredibly talented dick didn't go anywhere near that girl. She was blackout wasted. I spent the night on the sofa." He appraised me, realization dawning as he spoke. "It was some wanker who screwed her over, actually. I believe she said he was a tattoo artist."

I rubbed my hands over my face, trying to get my anger under control. "Blackout wasted?" Ree had been high. *Rejected* and high. I'd pushed her away, left her all alone to fend off the darkness in a strange city. Fuck.

Synner nodded. "And, inexplicably, not interested," he said. "Look, I don't need to *harass* non-consenting pussy. I have enough willing women to keep me busy for all eternity."

"He's telling the truth," Dash said, and I turned around to see that everyone else had gathered to watch our exchange. Great. "She just slept here. That's all." He took a step forward, nodding toward the front door. "We're out of milk. Time to go to the store—you and me."

What he really meant was, *Time to chill the fuck out, Dare.*

"Dash, we've got—" Indie began, but he cut her off with a stern look. "Fine," she said with an exasperated sigh. "Whatever. Everyone can just do whatever the hell they want today." She threw her hands up in the air. "I give up!"

Synner laughed and said something to her, but I couldn't make out the words because Dash had grabbed my elbow and was already dragging me out of the apartment.

"Damn," I muttered once we'd stepped onto the front porch, wrenching my arm from his tight grasp. "Now I know what it feels like to be a little brother. Painful as fuck."

"That's the first time I've ever heard you refer

to yourself as my little brother." He studied me, pressing his lips together as he gathered his thoughts. "Look, if I'd had any idea she was *your* Ree, I would've told you right away."

"I know." I gritted my teeth, feeling my wrath toward Synner dissipate. All I had left was anger at myself.

"Dare…" Dash's voice was low, his words barely audible. "I don't mean to preach, but you're fucking this up."

"I know." I sat down on the top stair.

Dash settled down beside me and stretched his legs out in front of him. "But it's not too late. I saw the way she looked at you."

"Ree…" I sighed, unable to get the rest of the sentence out. My chest ached, my head pounded. I took a deep breath and glanced over at Dash. "…has a problem."

He turned to look at me, his eyebrows knitting together at the look on my face. "A serious problem, I take it?"

"Pills," I said. "She can't function without them."

"Ree's an addict?" The word *addict* sounded so harsh and judgmental, even though there wasn't a hint of either in his voice.

I swallowed hard, but didn't respond. Saying *yes* would make it real, and I didn't want to label her.

"Things are good when we're together. She

doesn't use."

Doubt filled Dash's eyes. "Why do I sense a cosmic *but* coming up?"

"Because the moment her family enters the picture, her resolve shatters and she just…breaks. They OWN her, and they break her. Over and over again." Anger and frustration raged through my body, and I rubbed at the tightness in my jaw. "And she always gives in to them. She never lets me help."

"Is that what happened in Paris?"

I shook my head. "That's what happened in New York three years ago, and I could see it coming again. This time I didn't stick around to watch her bend to their will and then descend into the darkness that consumes her." And now I was kicking myself for it. I should've been there for her. I should've been her light.

Instead, I chose to be an asshole.

Dash didn't say anything. He didn't have to.

"I've been through this with my mom," I said, feeling the tightness in my chest expand. "Ree might be using pharmaceuticals and not smack, but drugs are drugs. You and I both know that." That was our joint family legacy. Thanks to our bastard father.

"We also know that it can be overcome." Dash had done it. He'd kicked the habit for good. But my mom hadn't gotten there yet.

My gut knotted. The mere thought that Ree could be like my mom and that I could be the cause of her downward spiral this time made me sick. It made me feel like my father—he'd always triggered my mom's relapses. He would do something—cheat, beat us, get arrested, kill someone—and she'd start chasing that mind-numbing high again.

"Seeing Ree so broken, losing her over and over again…it fucking kills me." My words were a hoarse whisper. "I can't let her sink."

"So don't." Dash placed a hand on my shoulder. "Help her. You've done it before. From everything Dalia has told me, your mom is only alive today because of you."

I shook my head. "But I haven't been able to fix her. My mom's good for a while, but then falls apart again. I'm a fucking failure, Dash."

He squeezed my shoulder. "You haven't failed. Your mom has to *want* to get better. She has to do the work. Her slips are not your fault. There is only so much you can do."

"What if I fail with Ree, too?" The idea was scary as hell. And also much too possible. "What if I can't help her?"

"Just be there for her, Dare."

"What if I'm not enough?"

He looked me straight in the eye. "You are. You already said she doesn't use when you two are together. You're enough, Dare. But you gotta stick with her. So stop fucking up."

He smirked and smacked the back of my head. Just like I always did with Dax. The more time I spent with him, the more he really felt like my brother.

"I love her, Dash." Stunned by my admission, I stared down at my hands, not quite believing what I'd just said. What the hell did I know about loving someone? My idea of love and family had been warped from day one. Sure, I loved my siblings, but that was different.

Ree, on the other hand, had blindsided me. She'd snuck her way into my mind and heart, and now refused to let go. Or maybe I wouldn't let *her* go. She was my addiction, but there was no twelve-step program to scrub her out of my system. There was no detox to remove her from my heart. She'd somehow become a living part of me—she WAS my fucking heart. We were the same. One whole.

"I know." Dash leaned forward, put his elbows on his knees, and looked down the street at the cars and people passing by. "But does *she* know that?"

Did she? We'd never said it to each other. Or, well, Ree had said it to me yesterday, but I'd totally ignored her words. I'd been too busy being an ass. Being my dad.

Fuck it all, I was not going to become like him.

"I haven't told her," I said, feeling like a Neanderthal. What had I been waiting for? Or maybe the better question was: why did three little words scare the shit out of me? That was ridiculous.

Of course, once upon a time, I'd sworn I'd never say those words to anyone because of what they'd done to my mom. Love ruined you. It made you weak. It made you need someone so much you couldn't function without them. I'd vowed I would never put myself in that position, that I wouldn't utter those words unless they were true…and that just wasn't going to happen.

Ever.

My mom had laughed at the time—during one of her sober periods when she shined like sunlight on water and things were so fucking good at home. Back when it seemed like we'd be okay—the four of us, Dax, Dalia, me, and mom—when we felt like a real family.

She'd put her arm around my shoulders and said with laughter in her voice that I hadn't heard since, "Oh, honey. You'll say it one day because you love so fiercely. And when you fall in love with the right girl, you won't be able to stop yourself. Trust me on this. It'll happen."

"Yeah right," I'd said. "When pigs fly."

She'd just shook her head and continued

laughing. "You mark my words, Daren. You'll meet her. And you'll love her with all your heart."

The kicker was…mom had been right.

"The Flying Pig," Dash said suddenly.

"What?"

"That's what she told the cab driver when I saw her off," he said. "It's a hostel downtown, not that far from your tattoo parlor actually."

"The Flying Pig." The irony wasn't lost on me, and I started to laugh. My mom would love that.

"Do you want me to come with you?"

I shook my head. "I've got it," I said as I rose to my feet. "I've got *her*."

Finally, I really and truly did. I only hoped it wasn't too late.

seven
Reagan

The sharp sting of hot water beating down on me felt soothing as it washed away the grime of last night, the stink of my shame. I leaned my forehead against the cold, wet tile of the shower stall. Now if only it could wash away my sins, both real and imagined. I knew what Dare thought, and I had to find some way to get him to understand that nothing had happened.

I'd already lost everything else. Without him, I had nothing left to fight for.

I knew what I had to do. I'd go to the tattoo parlor and explain. He'd have to listen to me. He'd have to believe me. The truth was on my side. That had to count for something, didn't it?

In most circumstances, the truth had value. It held importance and power. But in my experience—in my entire freaking life—it rarely mattered. Truth could be bought, words manipulated, promises broken. It could even be buried in the cold, hard earth. Or burned to ashes.

But Dare wasn't from my world. The rules of the game were different here. Truth meant something in his world—the REAL world.

At least I hoped it did.

The water had cooled so I turned it off, standing in place for a moment as I listened to the others chatter from their shower stalls. The droplets running in rivulets down my body were swallowed up by the thin towel I wrapped around my chest. Staying at a hostel was a completely different experience for me. Communal showers, communal kitchen, communal almost everything. But it was cheaper than a hotel, and considering I had no idea how long I going to be here, it made no sense to look for an apartment.

At least I'd gotten a private room so I could get away from people when I wanted to.

Everyone was pretty nice at least—mostly college students and people in their twenties who were traveling through Europe for the summer—though the amount of partying going on downstairs in the bar was too reminiscent of my old life, of the old Reagan.

As tempting as it was to go join them and drink myself into oblivion after the morning I'd had, I was trying really hard to resist. I couldn't go see Dare high or drunk. Not even tipsy. I had to show him I was willing to change if I was going to have any chance with him.

No matter how much I craved the escape of a pill right now, I craved Dare more.

I dried off, then slipped into a cool, white cotton sundress. My dark blonde hair hung long and wet down my back, and I squeezed the water out of it with the towel before combing it out. I didn't bother with makeup, just picked up my bag of toiletries and headed back to my room.

As soon as I stepped out of the women's bathroom, I glanced down the hall toward the front desk and froze.

His hands were thrust in his pockets, his hair a dark mess as he shifted his weight, his back to me. And I felt overwhelmed at his mere presence. Had he—

"Dare?"

He turned and looked at me as if I were the rain to his desert. Like he'd been searching for me his whole life and had finally found me.

But there was something else in his dark gaze, too. A sadness that ran deep. And I had no idea how to react, what he wanted of me, or what I could do to keep that amazing look on his face.

So I waited.

And hoped.

Dare didn't say a word; he simply closed the distance between us, pulled me into his arms, crushing me to him, fusing our bodies together as if he couldn't get close enough. I gasped at the intensity of his embrace, and matched it with my own.

"I'm sorry," he whispered in my ear, breathing me in, squeezing me even tighter against his chest. "I am so sorry, Ree."

His fingers threaded through my hair, and I wrapped my arms around his waist, locking us into each other. My entire body shuddered as I inhaled and slowly relaxed into him.

Oh, god. He'd come for me.

"I'm sorry, too," I said into his shirt. "For everything. But nothing happened with that guy. I sw—"

"I know." He pulled back and gently lifted my chin up so that my eyes met his. That look was still there—please god, let it never go away—and it took my breath away. His eyes trailed down to my lips and suddenly my whole body was on fire for him.

"I have a room upstairs." The words came out in a hoarse whisper.

Dare nodded, weaving his fingers through mine, letting me lead the way.

As we climbed the stairs, I could feel his eyes burning through the thin material of my dress, heating me up from the inside, making my body come alive again like only he could. I opened my door and he followed me inside, shutting it behind us. The sound of the lock turning made my heart skip a beat.

"Ree…"

I was too afraid to turn around and face him, to say anything that might make him run. All of my hopes and dreams soared. Little optimistic idiots. Didn't they know that Dare had the power to make them to crash and burn with a single word?

"Look at me, Ree."

I shook my head ever so slightly, blinking back the tears that stung my eyes. I couldn't fuck this up again. Whatever I said had to count. Dare had to know just how much I loved him. I had to make him forgive me, trust me, believe in me.

His footsteps were muffled by the carpet, but I heard him cross the cramped space. A rush of air hit my bare back as his hands gripped my shoulders. He turned me around, and my breath hitched at the overwhelming pain that splintered his eyes. Pain entwined with need and something so vivid, radiant, and powerful it nearly blinded me with its magnificence.

No one in the entire world had ever looked at me like that.

With love.

"Dare…I…" My heart squeezed as tears spilled onto my cheeks.

"Damn it, Ree." He grabbed my face in his hands, claiming my mouth with such need and haste I felt it in every part of my body and mind. I parted my lips and let his tongue in as he moaned into me.

My pulse raced. Blood rushed into my brain, making my head spin.

I was dizzy with Dare. Dizzy with desire. Dizzy with love.

His mouth was everywhere—sucking at my jaw, my neck, my collarbones, licking the valley between my breasts as he pushed the top of my dress down in search of my nipples. He was insatiable, untamed.

My world exploded. Nothing made sense.

Yet everything felt right.

Dare's hands fisted into my dress, pulling me closer. I clawed at his black t-shirt, tugging the material up over his head. He only let go of me to raise his arms, then his hands were back on me—in my hair, on my breasts, my waist, my thighs.

Demanding. Possessing. Owning.

Unable to contain my arousal, I cried out when his fingers dipped under my clothes, skimmed my soaked panties, and cupped my throbbing core. When he slipped them under the lace and stroked my folds, his thumb rubbing my clit, my hips bucked against his hand. Heat shot through me, unfurling every one of my deepest, darkest desires at once.

"God, you're so fucking wet." His voice was

rough and gravelly and the unabashed need in his words made my heart beat harder. The throb between my thighs pulsed with need, aching with want for him and him alone.

He picked me up so that my back pressed against the wall, and I wrapped my legs firmly around his waist. Every single muscle on every part of his body—arms, chest, abs, legs—was so tight and stiff as if he was trying to restrain himself from crushing me completely.

And all I wanted to say was, *Don't. Please don't hold back from me anymore.*

He bit his way along my collarbone and up my neck to the tender spot where my pulse hammered. Liquid heat flooded my veins and the throbbing between my legs got so strong I was sure I would come at any moment. And when he thrust his fingers into me, I almost unraveled. I moaned his name over and over again to the rhythm of the hard, wild strokes inside me.

Dare's eyes darkened perilously, and a low growl formed in his chest.

"You slay me, Ree," he said as he delved even deeper, faster, his fingers moving in and out while his thumb circled my clit. "You fucking slay me every single time. And I let you. I always let you."

The feeling was mutual.

He leaned forward and enveloped me with his body, his lips enclosing mine, his fingers curved inside me, coaxing me toward the edge as his other hand wrapped tightly around the back of my neck. My own hands couldn't rest. They sought out his hair, clawed at his back, gripped his muscular biceps.

I needed more of him. All of him.

ONLY him.

"I let you," Dare said, "because I love you." His fingers hit a spot inside my body at the same time as those words connected with my soul.

I exploded without warning, his name a cry on my lips. The tension that had built up over the past few weeks left my body as the orgasm quaked through me.

He didn't let me rest, didn't allow me to respond. Before the spasms had even subsided and without releasing my lips, he tore open his jeans and filled me with his hard length. We moaned in unison at the contact, connecting on a primal, desperate level that transcended the physical.

"I fucking love you and I can't help it." His voice strained as he pumped his hips, the sentence vibrating through me, its meaning echoing in the depths of my soul. "I can't stop. I don't want to." My breaths were reduced to ragged pants as bright white spots appeared behind my lids. I was soaring higher than ever before, my mind so full of his words and my body so full of him that I couldn't tell where he ended and I began. "Jesus, Ree. What have you done to me?"

His thrusts grew more demanding, consuming my cries, draining me of sanity. My head connected with the wall, and I sank my teeth into his lip.

Dare pulled back, groaning. "Shit. Am I hurting you?"

I shook my head, unable to speak.

The only pain I felt was the very real fear that he would somehow slip through my fingers now that I finally had him. Like every tiny piece of happiness in my life already had.

In this moment, Dare's rough movements were welcome. They made me feel alive. I needed the sharp sting of every bite and scrape of his teeth, wanted his fingers to keep digging into my hips, craved the wild grind of his pelvis as he pushed so deep into me. I felt every raw, unbridled thrust with great agony and even greater pleasure.

"Please don't stop," I said, begging not only with my words, but also with my body. "I love you, too. I always have."

Dare groaned and blazed a trail of kisses along my jawline and down my neck as his hips rocked in and out. Electricity built up anew in my core, each thrust bringing me closer to the edge of the highest cliff I'd ever climbed. Higher than any pill had ever taken me.

I held onto every part of him, my legs wrapped around his waist, my arms clinging to his neck, my muscles clenching his thickness as my eyes stayed firmly locked on his. Tingling centered between my thighs as we moved together, his heart throbbing in sync with mine, and I was suddenly calling out his name, my body exploding into a thousand fireworks, bright sparks engulfing my vision. Dare came with me, the *Ree!* he cried out a sound of pure love on his lips.

Pinned against the wall and bathed in our combined sweat and juices, I shuddered beneath him as our joint pleasure continued to course through us. Even once we both descended from the high, I tightened my grasp on him.

This wasn't an escape. It was real life. Dirty, gritty, magnificent.

Dare was mine.

I was his.

And I was never letting him go. Ever again.

eight
Dare

As we lay on the bed in her tiny hostel room, our bodies woven together and our breaths flowing in unison, all I could think about was the pain I'd seen in her eyes when she'd spotted me down by the front desk.

My heart had never hurt like this before. It had never cared so much for someone, nor been so deeply affected. Ree and I had started out as two fucked up, wounded parts who completed each other and made one another whole. But there was only so much pain two broken parts could stand before cracking. Eventually, healing had to take place.

I had to heal Ree. Or, really, I had to make her understand that she needed it.

I reached up and brushed a damp strand of hair off her face. There was a tiny spark of contentment in her eyes, but it was gone before it had a chance to light the rest of her face.

She sank her teeth into her lower lip. "What's wrong?"

"Ree…" Her name was just a whisper as I traced her jawline with my thumb, slowly making my way up to her lip so I could free it. I was about to cross into dangerous territory. One wrong word could make me lose her again.

Panic flooded her face—I needed to just spit it out.

"We can't keep doing this," I said quietly.

"Don't say that, Dare. Don't you fucking say that." She placed her hands on my chest and tried to push away from me, but I tightened my arms around her, keeping her close.

"Wait. Just listen." I took a deep breath. "Listen to me, please."

Fuck. This was going to be hard.

"You need help. Those pills will destroy you." I couldn't believe what I was doing, what I was saying. Every muscle in my body hurt from strain. I was wound so tightly, full of so many emotions. "I can't fix you. I wish I could, but I can't." I took a deep breath. "I've tried before…with my mom…but it's not—"

"I'm *not* like your mom." She squeezed her eyes shut and shook her head. "I can't believe you think that about me. I'm not a druggie." Her voice shook as she spoke. "I've never used those kinds of—"

"Drugs are drugs, Ree. It doesn't matter if it's

heroin or those pills you take. You need to learn to deal with life without them."

Her voice softened as she glanced up at me and said, "But, I'm fine when I'm with you." Her fingers brushed my cheek, soft and featherlight. "I'm always fine with you, Dare."

Goddamn it. It would be so easy to believe her. She was so fucking beautiful.

And beautifully broken.

"Except every time your family rears its ugly head."

"No, it's not like that—*I'm* not like that. I'm NOT an *addict*." Tears glistened in her eyes as she broke from my grasp and scooted up to the headboard, her knees pressing into her chest. "I'm NOT, I'm not, I'm not," she said, but with each *not* her voice got quieter and quieter as if she believed the words less and less. "I just...sometimes I just don't want to FEEL. That's all, Dare. I've stopped before. I don't need it when we're together. Not usually."

"Ree, listen to yourself," I said, not unkindly. "I've been through this. I've heard all the excuses. And I fucking *love* you. I've never said that to anyone before. I've never felt this with anyone. You are everything to me. Every-*fucking*-thing. I need you." I was in front of her now, wrapping my hands around her waist, pulling her onto my lap. "But you have to get well if we're going to work. Because we're never going to make it if you keep letting those pills rule your life. Look at everything that has happened already. That'll be our life if you don't get better. It will tear us apart." I pressed my forehead to hers, lowered my voice to a whisper. "I can't let that happen. I can't lose you ever again."

She shivered in my arms, her expression so wounded I expected her to flee. But she didn't.

"I don't know how to stop," she finally said, pressing her lips together. "I'm a fucking mess. Look at me."

"You're not a mess." I pressed my lips to her forehead. "You're my other half." I knew that without a shadow of a doubt. But no matter how much I wanted to, I couldn't be the one to fix her. Not entirely, anyway. I could be here for her while she fought her demons, help her get the help she so desperately needed. "I don't know how to make you stop either, but you can go someplace for help."

She stiffened. "Rehab?"

"There's a center right outside of town," I said carefully. "One of the artists at Vogel Tattoos stayed there last year for a bit. He's been clean for ten months."

Ree was quiet for a long while, lost in deep thought. Her eyes, though, never left mine. The blue hues of her irises were so uniquely distinct that no matter how many shades of paint I employed, I could never quite capture their true splendor. Right now, her gaze was as dark and turbulent as the restless ocean before an oncoming storm.

"I don't want to be like this anymore," she finally said, pressing her cheek to my chest. A wave of relief flooded me. "I don't want to be afraid or broken or weak. I want to be Real Ree."

Her words shook me to the core.

"You are real, Ree," I said. "And so fucking strong."

"Doesn't feel like it." She sounded small, lost.

"I know you can do this." I crowned her head with kisses. "It's only twenty-eight days, baby. That's all."

Her shoulders stiffened. "Twenty-eight days? A whole month without you?" She shook her head and started to pull away. "I don't know—"

"Not *without* me." I tightened my grip, keeping her safely locked in my grasp. "I'll be by your side the whole time. I'm not going anywhere. You won't be a prisoner there. You can leave whenever you like. And I can visit." I tilted her chin up so I could look in her eyes. "But it's important for you to stick it out if you're going to get better. *You* have to be the one to do this. If we're going to have a chance, you have to CHOOSE this."

"I do," she said slowly. "I'll go."

"Tomorrow."

"*Tomorrow?*" Once again, she stiffened. But a few seconds later, she nodded.

"I'll take you," I said, pressing my lips to hers. "It'll be okay. I promise."

Her arms instinctively wrapped around my neck as she returned my kiss. "Don't give up on me. Promise you won't."

"I won't." I cupped her face with both of my hands. "But you can't give up either."

She shook her head. "I won't."

I would be here for her. Waiting patiently.

Two parts, one whole.

Together, yet divided.

At least for now.

nine
Reagan

The first words out of Dare's mouth the next morning while I was packing up my stuff were: "Where is it?"

I swallowed hard. My bottle of pills. He didn't have to say it; I knew that was what he meant. And I knew what he wanted me to do with it.

I shut my eyes and took a deep breath. I could do this. I could say goodbye to my old friends, the one constant in my life for the past seven years.

Oh, dear god.

My hands were shaking when I picked it up, and I didn't even turn around to see if Dare was standing in the bathroom doorway. I knew what I had to do, no matter how fast my breaths came nor how hard my heart pounded.

But what if I wasn't strong enough to live without them? What if the nightmares came when Dare wasn't around? What if I couldn't face my past sober?

My life was about to be picked apart and then put back together. And while I was looking forward to the latter, I'd have been lying if I said the other didn't scare the living shit out of me.

I'd have to bare every one of my dirty secrets—to be heard, to be seen, to be judged.

Okay, I wasn't sure if I could do this.

Shit.

I turned to look at Dare standing behind me, and was taken at the love in his eyes. His strength ran through me, empowering me.

He believed in me, so I had to believe in myself.

I had to do this. For me. And for us.

I unscrewed the lid of the bottle and tipped out its contents. The pills cascaded into the toilet below. All of them.

Every. Single. One.

"Are there any more?" he asked quietly.

I shook my head, still staring as they sank to the bottom of the bowl in all their colorful glory. For years now, I'd only been able to function with their help—the uppers when I wanted to feel, and the downers when I needed to forget. I had no idea how I was going to survive without them.

My heart pounded even as I tried to calm myself.

It was going to be okay.

I was going to be okay.

Fuck it all, I could do this.

"I have to stop by the shop before we head out. Do you mind?" Dare said as he folded me into his arms. I clung to him, inhaling his scent, wishing I had a bottle of that to take with me.

It was only twenty-eight days.

I COULD DO THIS.

But did I mind delaying the start of that by a few hours? Nope. Not at all.

When we got to Vogel Tattoos, Dare disappeared into the back room in search of his boss while I sat in the waiting area and flipped through one of the well-worn black binders full of butterfly tattoo designs. Delicate to ornate, simple to highly detailed, and in every color imaginable, they were beautiful, though they paled in comparison to the radiance of my phoenix.

My phoenix. I wondered if Dare still had it. In everything that had happened, I'd totally forgotten to ask. And now that I no longer had my pills, I didn't know what I was going to do without my bird, how I would make it through the hell that was sure to follow in the next twenty eight days.

I started wishing I'd agreed to rehab AFTER I got my tattoo, because then at least I'd have it with me.

If he even still had the damn drawing.

Oh, god. He had to still have it.

A shadow fell over me and I ran my eyes up a pair of toned legs, a bare, pierced midriff, and tattooed arms, to Sia's face. I smiled at her and she sank down next to me on the deep red leather couch.

"So," she said, leaning forward, a cold, calculated look on her beautiful face, "I happened to overhear Dare telling Jasmine that he's taking you to Feniks Centrum." She widened her eyes and shook her head. "You poor thing."

Happened to overhear, my ass.

"Feniks Centrum?"

"The rehab center. *Feniks* means 'phoenix.' I'm sure it's supposed to be some great symbol of change." She rolled her eyes. "Like anyone actually *can* change. People don't, though, do they? Especially not addicts." She moved closer and lowered her voice to a whisper. "Hun, I've had SO many friends go through rehab and not one of them made it stick. Once an addict, always an addict. That's just the way things are, you know?"

God, what a bitch. But...what if she was right? My pulse sped up. What if this was all going to be a waste of time and money? This place wasn't cheap, and it was going to take all of the money I'd saved up to pay for my stay. When I got out, my bank account would be as empty as my parents' hearts. I'd have to start all over again.

Which would be fine…if the treatment worked. But if it didn't—*if I failed*—then I'd be out of money…and out of Dare. I knew there was no way he would stick around if I kept using. He'd made himself clear. No matter how much he cared for me, our love wouldn't be enough to withstand the devastation my addiction would leave in its wake.

I closed my eyes and leaned back against the couch, feeling the room swim. I couldn't lose him. Not again.

The name of the rehab had to be a sign. That was something I could cling to, even if I didn't have my drawing. Dare wouldn't have suggested this place if it didn't have a good success rate.

I opened my eyes to find Sia studying me.

"I can't believe you're doing this to him after everything he's had to endure with his mother."

"What?"

She shrugged her slight shoulders. "I mean, the guy just can't catch a break. First his whole childhood is spent dealing with a druggie mom and now his girlfriend is one. He must have a lot of bad karma he's working off." She tilted her head to one side as her dark eyes dimmed. "He deserves better than this. Better than *you*. I guess I had you pegged all wrong when we met yesterday."

"You know what? Fuck you." Goddamn it. I wasn't his mom. I would prove it to Dare, prove it to everyone. "You don't even know me, Sia. You have no right *pegging* me."

"You're right, I don't. But I do know Dare. VERY well. And I know that you're a selfish bitch to be putting him through this again."

"And you're a—"

"You ready to go, Ree?" Dare called as he came out of the back. Sia beamed up at him, stood, gave him a kiss on the cheek, and then shot me a nasty look. "Thanks for loaning me your car," he said to her as he held out his hand to me. "Ready?"

I watched Sia walk away, not even deigning to look over her shoulder at me, and then I stood up.

"As ready as I'll ever be," I said, but inside I was quaking.

Sia wanted Dare. That was clear as day. I'd gotten the feeling they had some sort of history when he'd first mentioned her three years ago, but it was obvious that for Sia it wasn't totally *history*.

And I was about to go away, while he'd be working with her. Side by side. Every day.

Fuck. Me.

What if he decided he wanted her instead? What if she convinced him that I'd never completely let go of the pills? What if she—

"Here." Dare held out a very familiar folded-up piece of paper, and I gasped at the sight of it in his hand. My phoenix. "Carry this with you—a piece of me that you can always have whenever you need it—and when the twenty-eight days are up, I'll start on the tattoo."

"Really?" My vision became blurry and my eyes stung as my fingers closed around it. "I won't be able to pay for—"

"Ree," he said, and I looked up into his fathomless dark eyes. "I'm doing it. You're not paying me for anything. *I'm* doing it. For *you*."

When Dare left me at the rehab center, I felt pure panic. I had my phoenix in one hand, my suitcase in another, but I had no idea what my life would be like twenty-eight days from now.

I had to finally face my past.

That, more than anything, scared the shit out of me.

ten
Dare

"Bloody hell. What did the poor toast do to you?" Synner hovered above me, watching me butter the bread. Or what was left of it.

Thirteen days without Ree. If I was a chick, I'd probably know the exact tally of hours, minutes, and seconds. That would definitely push me over the brink of insanity, especially considering I was already teetering on its edge.

He leaned down to take a closer look at my plate, then turned to me and said, "Did it fuck your girl, too?"

"Fuck. Off." I pointed the knife at his face. "I'm not above committing murder today. I'll happily live out my twenty to life here if it means shutting you up."

"You're not living here happily *now*," Synner said. "And I sincerely doubt that's going to change, if the last two weeks are any indication."

"I'd be a lot happier if you'd go away," I said,

still holding the knife out at him.

Indie walked into the kitchen and pushed the blade down toward the table. "Don't stab him Dare," she said, beelining for the coffeepot. "The guy is so perverted he might actually like it. Then you'll never get rid of him."

"You wish YOU'D never gotten rid of me," Synner said with a smirk. "Admit it. You miss the kink." He spanked her ass and reached into the back pocket of his jeans for his cigarettes.

Before he could pull one out, Indie had already smacked the pack out of his hand, sending it flying to the floor. "Not in the house," she said.

Synner groaned. "Why do you always insist on being such a bloody ice queen, Blue?"

Her lips parted and her expression softened the way it always did whenever he called her that. Then, just as quickly, it grew hard again. Synner grabbed for his smokes, and Indie rolled her eyes, though she didn't protest this time.

"Someone has to keep this band from sinking." She glanced over at the pink panty-clad ass peeking out from behind the open fridge door. "We're not running a bed and breakfast here, Synner," she said loudly enough for his groupie-du-jour to hear. "And even if we were—it's five o'clock in the afternoon."

Synner just calmly lit up, leaned back against the counter, and smiled at Indie. Then he raked his eyes over the girl's curves.

"She can't understand you. She doesn't speak English." He took a drag of his cigarette and licked his bottom lip. "But she screams just fine in Dutch."

Indie glowered. "All entertainment should've been long gone. We have a recording session in an hour."

"As if you didn't have some bloke in your room last night." Synner tucked the pack back into his jeans.

"Yeah," she said. "And he left. *Last night.*"

I tuned out their bickering, focusing on the piece of toast in front of me. It tasted like cardboard. Everything I'd eaten in the past two weeks had tasted like fucking cardboard. It didn't help that my stomach was knotted up to hell.

I was waiting for the call—the one that my mother had made so many times. *I can't do this, Daren. I'm not strong enough.*

I shook my head.

Ree wasn't my mom.

She was strong. She could do this. I just wished I could be by her side every step of the way. She felt too far away, too inaccessible.

A high-pitched giggle drew my attention toward Dash and the dark-haired girl he was kissing goodbye at the front door.

Once she'd cleared out, my brother pulled up a

stool at the breakfast bar. "That was Anouk," he said with a wicked grin. "Or maybe Aya?"

"Trying to fuck someone out of your head, too?" I threw the remainder of my toast down on the plate and wiped my hands on my jeans. "You know that doesn't work, right?"

He shrugged one shoulder and scratched at his chest—right at the spot of his newly inked wren tattoo. "Sure. But at least it's hell of a lot of fun to try."

But when he said it, he looked like he was trying to convince himself more than anyone else.

It had to be a girl. For the four years I'd known him, I'd never seen him like this.

"What did she do to you, anyway? The wren, I mean."

His jaw tightened as he broke eye contact. "Nothing," he said. "She's off limits."

Christ. We shared DNA, but sometimes it seemed like not much else.

"How's Ree?" Dash said, changing the subject.

I shrugged. "I have no fucking clue." I ran a hand over my face and sighed. "They insisted on no contact and no visitors for the first two weeks." Detox from everything, they'd said.

Detox. I knew all too well the havoc that could wreak. The girl I loved was going through hell right now. And there was nothing I could do to help.

"I get to visit tomorrow," I said. Finally.

The problem was, a single day felt like an eternity right now. Twenty-four of the longest fucking hours of my life. Every second was dragging so slowly I was pretty damn sure I was never going to make it through this day.

"Fuck it." I pushed away from the table with a growl. "I'm going to work."

Dash cocked his head to the side and arched a dark eyebrow at me. "Aren't you off tonight?"

"Not anymore," I said. "I need the distraction."

"Just like Vogel." Jasmine shook her bright red dreads when I showed up at the shop unannounced. "Living life one heartbeat at a time." For a lady in her sixties, she could still rock the hippie look.

"I need to work tonight," I said. "Give me whoever you've got." I didn't care how many girly butterflies she threw my way. I just needed something to do.

If I'd had a place to paint, I would have gone there instead. For the past two weeks, my hands had itched for a brush, my senses had craved the feel and smell of paint and turpentine.

If I could paint, I could lose track of time. I wouldn't spend every minute wondering whether the phone was going to ring for me. And the remaining two weeks of rehab could fly the fuck by. But I'd left all my stuff at my apartment in Paris. I'd been so intent on being a total jackass and getting away from the woman I loved, that I hadn't brought any of it with me.

Served me right.

Tattooing was as close to my art as I could get right now. I didn't have a brush, but a gun. And human bodies were my canvases. Paint and ink became one and the same.

Somewhat.

"I'm on my way out, darling," Jasmine said, coming around her table and blowing me a kiss as she walked by. "It's been slow for a Friday and Sia is the only one left at the show. Maybe she needs a hand with something."

Ever since I'd been here, Sia had needed a hand with something. As long as I was at work, I had a shadow. I'd kept my distance as best I could—I didn't want her getting the wrong idea just because we had a history.

Now, as I wandered back to her station, I saw her bending over some guy, adding color to the sleeve covering the upper half of his arm.

When she glanced up and saw me, her entire face lit up.

Once that would have meant something to me. When we'd first met at Rex's studio in Brooklyn, she'd been this tough chick from the Bronx who'd grown up in foster care and didn't take shit from anyone. Especially not the screw-up fresh out of juvie.

Older and more experienced, she'd wanted nothing to do with me, had done her best to convince me that I'd never amount to anything. *Once a convict, always a convict*, she'd said to me. And I'd listened. My life had been one failure after another, and I knew she was right. What was the point of trying if I was just going to keep failing?

But then Rex had put a brush in my hand and told her to sit for me.

She'd done it because she worshipped Rex.

He and I had painted her, side by side, day after day. Once in a while he'd look at my canvas and point out where the shadows were off or the shape was wrong, but for the most part he'd left me to do my own thing.

Sia had changed when she'd seen my painting. It wasn't finished yet when I found her looking at my canvas, the cloth flipped up so she could see the whole thing. She'd stared at me wide-eyed for a moment, her mouth agape.

All I could think at the time had been, *Was it really that bad?*

Then she dropped her robe, wrapped her exotic, naked body around me, and latched on. She didn't let go until she left for Amsterdam six months later.

That had been years ago and, in that time, everything had changed. Including me.

"I'm here," I said to Sia now as she hunched back over the guy's beefy arm. "If anyone else comes in, I'll take them." She nodded, and I went to my workspace to prepare it just in case.

Because, *goddammit*, someone needed to come in and get a tattoo soon. Hell, I was going to go out on the street and drag them in here kicking and screaming if I needed to.

Twenty minutes later as I was wiping down my chair, I felt Sia's arms wrap around my waist and her hips slide up against my ass.

My head whipped up, and I flinched away. "What the hell are you doing?"

"What does it look like, Dare?" She slinked toward me, slipping the strap of her tank top off her shoulder. "We're all alone. Why don't we have a little fun together?" She took another step forward and began playing with the other strap. "Just like we used to."

I shook my head. "No, thanks."

"Oh, come on, Dare." She pouted. "It's you and me. Remember how good we were together? How fucking hot things could get? We could be like that again."

"Sia, that was a fling. It was…nothing."

She froze, her eyes narrowing. "It wasn't *nothing*. Not to me."

"You sure about that?" I crossed my arms over my chest. "You left the country pretty easily as I recall. Rex said 'Amsterdam' and you jumped at the chance."

"That was six years ago. Things are different now."

"You're right," I said with a nod. "They are. I'm with Ree now."

"*Ree.*" Sia rolled her eyes. "Always Ree. You haven't stopped talking about her since the day she walked through that door."

"I love her, Sia."

A fire ignited in her eyes. "You don't do love, Dare."

"I do with Ree." The ease of that statement startled me.

Loving Ree was simple and complicated, freeing and intense. It was everything I was meant to do. It was my reason for taking this breath and the next.

And I couldn't stand another minute without her.

Ree stirred in her sleep as I slowly shut the door to her room, the squeak of its hinges way too loud in the silence of the rehab center after lights out. I snuck over to her bed and sat down, my gaze immediately drawn to her.

She lay on her side with arms tucked to her

chest, her long, silky hair fanning out around her like a golden halo. Her lips were slightly parted as she let out a small sigh, and the peaceful look on her face caused me to relax a little. I brushed my fingers across her cheek, then traced her mouth with my thumb.

Before she even opened her eyes, she said, "Dare?" Her voice was gravelly and slow with sleep, my name on her lips so fucking sexy. The corners of her mouth quirked up, and more tension left me after hearing yet another contented sigh.

She was okay. She was safe, smiling, and still mine.

"God, I've missed you, Ree." I wanted to dig my hands into her hair, devour her, breathe her in, and fill myself up with her. Leaning over, I planted a soft kiss on her forehead.

Her lashes fluttered, and she looked up at me with a sweet, drowsy smile. "Am I dreaming? Are you real?"

"Not a dream," I said with another kiss. "Real Dare. And Real Ree."

Even in the dimness, she managed to be the light. Her eyes were brighter, clearer, and more focused like she was totally present in the moment. Completely with me. Thank god.

"How did you get in here?" she asked as I slid onto the bed, her arms winding around my waist, making me feel like myself again.

"I seduced the sexy nurse," I whispered into the sweet smell of her hair.

She let out a groggy laugh and pulled me closer. "What about the burly security guard?"

"No. I tried, but he was immune to my charms," I said quietly.

She slugged me gently. "I'm serious."

"Come on, Ree. I spent a year and a half in juvie, remember? A guy doesn't leave a past like that behind without *some* skills." I pulled her close, melding my body to her thin frame, entwining my legs with hers. "I had to sneak in. I couldn't take another minute without you."

"Nor me you," she said as she nestled her head in the crook of my neck.

We fell asleep like that, tangled together as one.

Like we were always meant to be.

eleven
Reagan

Waking up in Dare's arms this morning was my reward for living through the torture of the past fourteen days.

The first week, I barely slept, had nightmares when I did, and experienced panic attack upon panic attack in therapy sessions. My palms were constantly sweaty, I was bitchy to everyone, and I couldn't stop shaking for days.

The second week, I began to talk. Word by word, sentence by sentence.

There were countless times I wanted to walk out the door. And even more times I wanted to reach for my pills to just dull the pain. Because everything hurt—mind, body, and soul. There were days when I couldn't imagine it ever getting better, when I wondered why the fuck I was putting myself through all this.

But I held on to my phoenix, my little piece of Dare, clutching it in my hand when the darkness came and the pain became too much to bear. And when he crawled in my bed last night and curled up beside me…everything else faded away.

His arm tightened around me now when he felt me stir, and I snuggled closer against him, inhaling his familiar scent. Even without his paints and canvases, he still smelled like art. I melded myself into the arc of his body, reveling at how perfectly we fit together.

Two parts, one whole.

Still. Thank god.

I slid my hands along the warm, smooth skin of his arms, and laced my fingers with his.

"You're staying today, right?" I said.

He flashed me a sleepy grin. "You couldn't get rid of me if you tried."

My entire body relaxed at his words, and I sank into him, smiling, trusting that he really was here to stay. With me. Forever.

I needed to believe this. Especially today.

Rolling onto my back, I turned to look up at him. "Will you come to group therapy with me?"

His eyebrows shot up and his eyes widened. "You want me to?"

I nodded. Part of this treatment was not only examining your own demons, but also sharing them with people you trusted. People who didn't send you into a downward spiral, but who pulled you back up. Dare was my people. My ONLY one.

"They'll let me sit in?" he asked.

Once again, I nodded. "There's a family and friends session at noon," I said. "Now that my detox is up, they recommend inviting loved ones to sit in. I'd really like it if you came."

Initially, I hadn't told Dare about it because I wasn't sure if I'd be strong enough to brave a meeting between him and my monsters. But we had to start somewhere if we were to have a real shot at a future.

I extracted myself from his arms—reluctantly, but the day was starting and we had to stick to a schedule at the center. It was another component of the treatment, of the new lifestyle I had ahead of me.

I took a quick shower and got dressed in the bathroom, suddenly feeling a little shy around Dare. My hands shook as I toweled off. There were things he would learn about me today that I had no idea how he would handle. I'd been conditioned by my parents to believe I was the cause of all my problems. The blame always lay with me. I was aware now that wasn't true, but the self-hate was still embedded deep within me. Yanking it out was a long process.

When I came out of the bathroom, Dare was standing by the window, already dressed.

"Ready?" I asked.

"For you? Always."

We sat next to each other, but I didn't touch him. I couldn't even look at him. My entire body felt wound as tight as a freaking yo-yo, and my emotions were about as stable as one. We listened to people testify about their breakthroughs and setbacks. Only a couple of others had someone else with them, and I was amazed at how openly they spoke in front of these new strangers, Dare included.

I was going to have to do it, too.

Oh, god.

"Reagan?" Gino, the counselor, was pointing at me. "What about you? Do you have anything you wish to share today?"

My mouth felt dry, and when I tried to speak no sound came out. I cleared my throat and reached deep inside for every little piece of resolve I could muster. "I'm…uh…" I glanced at Dare and was struck silent by the look of pride on his face.

Pride? He was *proud* of me?

No one had ever looked at me like that. And he was doing it here of all places, under these circumstances.

I was filled to the brink with warmth. And renewed strength.

"I'm doing better," I said, turning back to the

group. "I actually slept last night, and without nightmares of…" I swallowed hard, before forcing the word out. "…*Jackson.*"

"That's great progress, Reagan. I'm so glad to hear that." Gino smiled warmly at me, and I exhaled, feeling myself relax a tiny bit more.

Step one was done and over with. Despite being hard, it hadn't broken me.

Maybe I really could do this after all.

Dare and I sat in the circle of chairs after everyone else had cleared out to get lunch, but I could feel the questions burning in him and I knew I needed to get this over with before I'd be able to even think about food.

He'd stiffened when I'd said Jackson's name, then reached for my hand and held it tight as Gino moved his attention to someone else. The gesture had brought tears to my eyes, even as my stomach clenched at the thought of telling him.

But I had to. He needed to know.

And, maybe more importantly, I needed to tell him.

"So," he said when we were finally alone. "Jackson?"

I nodded, inhaling sharply.

"If you don't want to talk about it right now," he said quickly, "it's okay, Ree. I'm here whenever you're ready."

Shaking my head, I said, "No. I want to. It's just...hard." I pushed the tears back down. I couldn't allow this to keep making me fall apart. I was tired of the control my history had over me. It was time to assert myself over my past. Finally. Once and for all.

Or, at least, one step at a time.

"Jack..." God, my heart beat too fast, my breathing came too quick. I was going to pass out if I didn't get my body under control. I pressed one hand to my chest in an effort to calm down.

It was going to be okay. *I* was going to be okay.

Jackson wasn't here.

"He...attacked me."

I chanced a glance at Dare. His jaw was tight, his fists clenched, and his eyes glued to my face. But there was no judgment in his expression. No disgust. No disbelief. Nothing that even remotely resembled the looks on my parents' faces when I'd told them.

I took another deep breath and pressed on.

"It was at a party my parents threw for his father—who was running for governor at the time. I'd gone down into the wine cellar to find a special bottle my father wanted...and Jack followed me."

Reagan...beautiful, beautiful Reagan.

Memories of that night flittered into my mind.

The lights going off in the cellar, sending me tumbling into darkness. The smell of the sweat on his skin mixing with the alcohol on his breath. The scent overwhelmed me in the damp, dark basement when Jack had come up behind me and whispered in my ear.

Shh, shhhh. I'm here. No need to cry. I'm going to give you what you've been asking for all night.

I heard the fucking grin on his face even as my skin crawled and my heart froze at the threat in his voice. Then his iron grip was suddenly around my arms, his erection already pressing into my back.

I've seen you watching me, Reagan. At school and tonight. I know you want me. I know you want this.

And then...

"How old were you?" Dare's voice was tight, tortured.

I looked down at my hands, unable to stand the agony etched on his face. "Fifteen. He was a senior."

Dare groaned as if he were in pain, and shot up out of his chair, sending it flying backward. I could feel the anger radiating out of him as he stormed over to the window, and I half expected him to smash the glass panes. Instead he yelled "FUUUUUUCK!" at the top of his lungs, his chest heaving.

Then he turned and, before I knew it, was

across the room, kneeling at my feet, his hands clutching mine, his eyes misty and brimming with so many raw emotions I couldn't even identify them all.

"I would kill him if I could," he said. "Hell, I *will* kill the bastard if I ever get the chance. I'm so sorry, Ree. For everything that happened. For everything he did. I'm so fucking sorry."

Tears rolled down my face and I reached forward to touch his cheek. He leaned into my hand and kissed my palm, his expression so dark and devastated I could physically feel his agony.

"Why are *you* sorry?"

"Because you didn't deserve it," he said. "You didn't deserve what that piece of shit did."

I lost it at those words, letting the tears spill out of me. Dare wrapped his arms around my waist and I hugged his head to my chest, sobbing out my relief at his acceptance along with all the years of hurt I'd been holding in.

When I'd told my parents about the attack, their first reaction had been disbelief, telling me I was being overly dramatic and making things up, fabricating a lie much worse than what had actually happened. They'd said I couldn't go around making up stories about the future governor's son just for attention.

But then when the evidence of what he'd done grew to be undeniable…they'd said it was my own fault. My skirt had been too short, my shirt too tight. I'd flirted with him too openly, smiled too much, given him the wrong idea. I'd let him do it, I obviously hadn't said *no* and afterwards I must have panicked and regretted it.

I was a slut. A whore. A disappointment to my family. A stain on the McKinley name.

My shame was complete.

And in a single sentence, Dare had blown that all away.

I never imagined I would have someone in my life who would love me no matter what. Someone who would see the good in me even when I couldn't. Someone who would choose to believe me even when the truth was a horror.

I'd never known what I was missing until Dare.

twelve
Dare

I stared out of the small window in Ree's room, feeling like I was suffocating. I had never harbored this much hatred toward someone in my life.

Pure, raw hatred.

Any guy who'd force himself on a woman wasn't a real man. He wasn't even a fucking human being.

Rage built up like a tight fireball in my chest, spreading into every crevice of my body and mind. I tried my damnedest to rein it in, if only to not wake Ree.

We'd come back to her room, curled up on her bed, and I'd held her until she fell asleep. Then I'd gotten up and worn a path the length of her room.

Fifteen. She'd been a fucking kid. She hadn't even—

FUCK. If I ever got my hands on that bastard

he wouldn't make it out alive.

Imagining that happening to Ree was killing me. That animal had crushed her spirit, beaten her down, stolen not only her innocence, but also her beautiful smile.

I wanted to murder him. No, TORTURE, then murder him.

And then I'd take care of her parents and make those sadistic assholes pay for their sins. They'd refused to acknowledge her pain, instead choosing to just drug the fuck out of her until she was numb to the world.

My heart felt like it was going to rip its way right out of my chest.

She'd had to carry this pain for seven years. All alone.

Seven *fucking* years.

No wonder she'd needed the escape the pills provided.

And hadn't I failed her, too? I hadn't been there three years ago when she'd needed me. I'd been so messed up myself that I'd failed to see the danger signs. She'd been hurting then. Why hadn't I stuck it out?

My fist connected with the window frame, rattling it. Ree startled, her eyes flew open, and I immediately felt like an ass.

"Shit. I'm sorry."

"Are you angry?" she asked, her voice barely

audible.

Angry? I was fucking livid. But I stuffed that down because she didn't need my anger right now. She just needed me. I could never undo what this monster had done. But at least I could be by her side.

I walked over to the bed and sat down, leaning over to gently brush the matted hair from her beautiful face. Blue eyes the color of the ocean searched mine, worry clearly reflected in their depths.

"At you? No. Of course not," I said, feeling my rage fading with each second I gazed at her.

Was that what love was all about? The ability to have another person's mere presence pluck you from hell and bring you back to earth with a single glance? I had no clue, but Ree had forced me to face emotions and acknowledge feelings I hadn't even known existed.

"I'm broken, Dare." Her eyebrows drew together and her forehead crinkled.

"You're beautiful, Ree." I smoothed the worry from her face, tracing my fingers over her cheek and along her jawline, reveling in the sensation of her silky skin under my fingertips. "The most beautiful woman I've ever known."

She shook her head and I searched the room, trying to think of some way to convince her. My eyes landed on a notebook lying on top of her nightstand.

"Let me show you what I see when I look at you," I said as I reached for it, also snatching the pencil that was off to its side.

I flipped to a blank page and focused on her face. I knew it better than I knew my own, having committed to memory every line and each curve long ago.

She stared up at me with so much need in her liquid gaze. "What do you see, Dare?"

"Your eyes that notice light even when the world is submerged in darkness," I said, sketching the arc of her eyelids, the contours of her eyes, the pencil in my hand an extension of my fingers and heart. "Eyes that find beauty in works of art that other people miss. Eyes that always perceive the best in me."

Her lips parted slightly and she drew in a shuddering breath as my pencil strokes got longer, freer.

"Your thick, golden hair that I love to run my hands through. Hair that always smells like honey and summer—like my Ree."

Her eyelashes fluttered and her head slowly fell back. I reached over to wrap my fingers around the soft, dark blonde strands that fell on her neck.

"Keep talking," she said in a whisper. "Please don't stop."

My fingers glided over to the velvet of her lips.

"This lush, sexy mouth that has called me some of the best things in the world. But also some of the worst."

Her lips quirked upward under my touch. "Sometimes you *can* be such an ass." A small laugh licked my fingers. "But you're MY ass, Dare Wilde."

She was smiling. Thank god.

"I am yours," I said. She fucking owned me. Her words had the power to make and break me. Her tongue darted out to taste my thumb, and I groaned. Damn, the things she could do to me. I craved to hear those soft lips moan my name.

Right now.

But I couldn't push her, so I focused back on the sketch. It didn't need my attention. Not really, anyway. I could draw Ree with my eyes closed.

I made my way down her neck—both with my look and my touch—pausing at her collarbone. It was more pronounced than usual. She'd lost weight over the past two weeks, weight she couldn't afford to lose. That alone told me how hard she'd had it.

"This is one of my favorite spots." I traced the protruding bones with my left index finger as the pencil in my other hand made a perfect replica on the paper in front of me. "A sweet spot I love to kiss and lick and bite." My voice was low and gravelly, thickened by primal hunger. "A spot I like to mark as mine."

"*Yours.*" She sounded relieved. And it broke my heart.

"Mine, Ree," I said. "Always. Forever."

"You still want me?" It was a half-statement, half-question.

Did I *still* want her? She had to be fucking kidding me. I'd never wanted anyone MORE than I wanted her.

"Of course I want you," I said. "But you have no idea how fucking badly I NEED you."

Her eyes widened and her cheeks tinted crimson, as if suddenly shy. But then she cleared her throat.

"Show me," she said, more a demand than a plea. "Show me how badly you need me, Dare."

Shit, she didn't have to ask twice.

My fingers wound around the back of her neck, and I pulled her into a kiss that was fueled by my need to consume her. Screw restraint. She needed convincing. My tongue parted her lips, ravenously greeting hers as I plunged deep into the warm softness of her mouth. A shudder ran through me when I heard a sweet, sultry moan vibrate deep in her throat. My blood pounded in my veins as that moan grew louder and morphed into the sound of my name.

Jesus. *Fucking.* Christ.

"I'll never stop needing you, Ree." I deepened

our kiss and she reached under my shirt, running her fingers down my abs—*goddamn*—and lower still, where she could feel the hard evidence of just how much I needed her.

"I'm not done making sure you know how beautifully perfect you are," I said, pulling away despite how much I wanted to keep going. "Not yet." I had no idea how I'd managed to pant my way through a full sentence. Or how I was achieving this level of self-control.

But this had to happen. She HAD to know.

I sketched the curve of her body. "This heart has so much more strength and power that you're not even aware of yet. It's the heart of an art lover. The heart of a woman who's been to hell and back, but still stands tall. A heart that's been broken and shattered, but still beats loud."

"For you." Her eyes were glassy with tears, but she was smiling. Her real smile. "Wait," she said. "I want to do this right."

"What…" The question died on my lips as she lifted her cherry-red tank top over her head.

Damn.

Two long weeks of agony and desire swam to the surface, threatening to erupt. I forced my mind—and my cock—to chill the fuck out.

"Draw me properly," she said as she slowly peeled off her bra. "Like one of your French girls." She dropped the lacy garment on the bed and laughed—the sound crystal clear, and so carefree and light. A sound I'd rarely heard from Ree. True happiness.

Something deep inside my chest stirred, my own laughter echoing hers. "Hell, don't you know the only one I cared about painting in Paris was you?" More seriously, I added, "You're my muse, Ree. Have been for three fucking years."

I hadn't stopped drawing her since the day we met. When I fled to L.A., when I was in Paris, she'd always come with me. If only in my mind and on my canvas.

In paint, she'd always been mine.

I bit back a tortured groan as she leaned against the metal bars of the headboard, arching her back, parting her lips, her sapphire eyes partially hooded by long lashes. That look wasn't meant for my heart. It was a message for another part of me. A part that stirred and throbbed at the sight of her.

Swallowing hard, I sketched her, desperately wishing my tongue was to her skin as the pencil was to the paper.

Drawing nudes was work. ART. I did it because I found limitless beauty in the human form, had fallen in love with its ever-changing nature, the way light and shadow could transform it even over the course of a day. I liked capturing it in paint, highlighting the uniqueness of body shapes and facial features. It wasn't about sex at all, like so many people assumed.

Sketching Ree, on the other hand, this intimately, this closely, this IMPORTANTLY wreaked havoc on me. It tested my limits, made me insane.

She was undoing me.

And—*to hell with it all*—I let her. Again.

And I was about to make it worse. And better. All at once.

"I can't see all of you," I said, placing the notebook down.

My eyes trailed down her body to her lap. To her skirt.

Her smile grew, turning into a smirk as she tugged the fabric over her hips and down her legs. "How about now?"

"Nope. Not yet." I shook my head, stretched across the bed, and hooked my fingers in the waistband of her panties. Instinctively, her hips rolled forward, letting me peel off the red lace.

Any other day, I'd be ripping it off. With my hands, my teeth, whatever. But today wasn't any other day. Today, I had to make her understand just how fucking perfect every part of her was.

I took my time, reveling in her nakedness, caressing the light tan of her creamy skin, drinking in her sweet, intoxicating scent. I almost lost it when my hand grazed her core, the evidence of her arousal glistening on my fingertips. My eyes never leaving hers, I licked her off of me, savoring her taste, coveting more of it.

I was an addict, too, after all.

And a single taste of Ree wasn't enough.

I craved more of her. I wanted to devour all of her.

Piece by piece. Kiss by kiss. Touch by touch.

I leaned forward so I could start the feast at her mouth, pressing my lips against hers as I wound my fingers through her golden mane. She responded without hesitation, her body melding against mine, her arms wrapping around my back to first tug my shirt over my head, then pull me even closer.

"I'm never letting you go," she whispered against my mouth, each word punctuated by a kiss. "Never again, Dare. I promise." Her nails raked over my back, digging in with more possessiveness than I had ever seen from her before.

Ree's need was palpable—a tangible thing I could practically reach out and grasp. It hummed through her every kiss, vibrated off her lips in waves, and cascaded into my waiting mouth, filling me.

She whimpered when I broke contact, but her breath quickened again as I began gently kissing up her jawline. I paused at her ear, so she could hear my own ragged breathing, so she could witness the effect she had on me. I bit down gently on the lobe, pulling on it softly, coercing a moan from deep within her.

Alternating between my lips and teeth, I worked my way down her neck and across her chest. Cupping her breast with my right hand, I circled her nipple with my tongue, playfully flicking and licking my way to the sensitive peak as my left thumb and forefinger teased its twin.

Before long, Ree was gasping and arching her back, pressing with greater urgency against my lips. When my mouth finally latched on, she cried out and dug her nails into my back. The already tight bud turned hard between my lips as I nipped at it with my teeth. Her gasps grew to sensual, throaty moans as her body quaked beneath me.

I continued to lick and bite at her breasts, slowly trailing my hand down her abdomen, across her stomach, along the edges of her hips, claiming the beautiful curves I had sketched just moments before. The instant I slid my hand over the top of her thigh, I felt her knees part.

Tempting me, taunting me, teasing me.

Unable to hold back my need for her any longer, I slid my hand between her legs.

Shit. Already soaked. "You are so fucking beautiful, Ree."

I cupped her with my palm and rubbed along her soft folds before dipping into her heat. One finger. Then another. First slowly—*excruciatingly*—then gradually faster and harder.

Ree cried out, then threw a quick glance at the door. "Oh, god. I don't think THIS is allowed here," she said, her eyes gleaming wickedly. "You're going to get me in trouble, Dare."

"Think of this as physical therapy." I kissed my way down her stomach and grinned up at her as I settled between her legs. "My contribution to the program."

With my fingers rhythmically pulsing inside her, I slowly licked my way to her clit. Circling it with my tongue, I flicked the sensitive bundle of nerves before claiming it with my lips and teeth. Ree screamed my name, then quickly clamped her hand over her mouth, shaking with laughter.

Her happiness was so beautiful…and such a fucking turn on.

"Keep smiling, Ree," I said, licking slowly, watching her arousal spike. "I don't ever want you to lose that happy smile." Her mouth formed a sensual O as she moaned, her hips rocking against my mouth. "Except when you're doing *that*." She bit her lip and let out a pleased groan that went straight to my cock. "And that. That is allowed, too."

Holy hell.

"Oh, god." Her fingers tugged at my hair. "What if someone hears and comes in?"

"We have an excuse," I said between tastes. "I'm an artist. I paint nudes. You're...*posing* for me." I let the words vibrate against her soft skin before adding, "Now lie back, relax, and let me fucking paint you. With my tongue."

The threat of getting caught quickly forgotten, Ree begged me not to stop. Over and over again, she pleaded with me...harder...faster...MORE. Increasing the pressure of my tongue, I savored the taste of her, the soft feel of her velvety skin, her sweet scent that radiated from every pore. My dick throbbed against the denim of my jeans while I coaxed her higher and higher, stroking and licking her into a frenzy, feeling like I would explode at any moment.

Ree tensed, and I felt her approaching her peak. So I gave her more. Harder. Faster. Relentlessly, madly, deeply. I was making love to her. With my fingers and mouth. And it was hot as hell.

Her breathing grew ragged and my name became a sexy moan on her lips as she tumbled over the edge, her legs trembling while the orgasm rocked through her body. Her sweet release spilled over into my mouth, and I continued to drink every single spasm from her, wanting to prolong her pleasure for as long as she'd let me.

Just when I thought she was thoroughly depleted, she looked down at me with wild eyes, threaded her fingers through my hair, and tugged. "I need you," she said, taking my bottom lip between her teeth. "More of you." Her fingers found my zipper and released me. "All of you." Her hand wrapped around my cock. "Just you." Slowly, she began moving. "*Please*, Dare."

FUCK.

Up. Down. Up. Down.

Pleasure ripped through me, setting my world on fire, scorching my mind until all common sense was burned to a crisp.

Breathe, Dare. Fucking breathe.

I didn't know how much more I could take. I had to have her. Right fucking now.

Hooking my hand under her leg, I lifted her so that she was straddling me, my rock-hard erection pressing impatiently against her. She moaned, kissing me urgently while grinding against me, her nails digging into my thighs, spurring on my need. I lifted my hips, and she rose to her knees, guiding me into her opening.

Jaw tight, teeth gritted, I filled her.

Inch by tight inch. Groan by hard groan.

All the while, I focused on her and only her. Those beautiful eyes swimming with lust. That soft smile playing across her lips. The erotic curves of her body.

The piece of art that was Ree.

"Oh, god." Her head fell back and she

practically sang my name as her muscles contracted around me, taking me in further, pulling me deeper.

My hands slid over her ass before settling on her hips, directing her to set the pace she needed. I surrendered control, worshipping her as she rode me, savoring this moment.

I wanted to show her what it meant to be loved.

She deserved love.

So much fucking love.

"I don't ever want this to stop," she said as if she'd read my mind.

"Then keep moving, baby."

She pulsed up and down, first slowly, then faster and faster until we were both breathing heavily. Giving her full control of this moment was a test of will.

Her legs quivered, and her eyes rolled back in her head, the air around us thick and heavy with sex and freedom. Every sultry moan spilling from her lips confirmed we were each other's missing half.

Two parts. One whole.

One hand still on her hip, my other climbed to her chest, claiming her heartbeat as I possessed her from the inside out. The move—combined with my length breaching a nerve-filled territory—pushed her over the edge with the sweetest sound I'd ever heard, and I exploded with her, pleasure engulfing us as she broke apart, crumbling against me, trusting me to cushion her fall. Just like she had that very first night we'd spent together.

I pushed her hair out of her face as she continued to tremble on my chest. "You know what else I see when I look at you?"

"A thoroughly satisfied girlfriend?" We were speaking in pants, our breaths one and the same.

Girlfriend. We'd never used that word before. Ree was beyond *girlfriend* for me.

That realization was like a blast of endorphins to the heart.

"I see a phoenix," I said. "A woman who rose from the ashes and is going to conquer the entire fucking world one day."

thirteen
Dare

Two weeks later, I was on day twenty-seven without Ree and my own detox was failing miserably. There was no way in hell I could get her out of my system.

Nor did I want to.

Not anymore.

Though we spoke on the phone nightly and I drove out to visit every Sunday, we hadn't been able to sneak in a repeat performance in her room. I missed the feel of her, the smell of her, the thrill of her mere presence.

And I missed drawing her.

Once I'd put pencil to paper again after so many weeks without it, I was going crazy to get back to my art. I hadn't said anything to her yet, but was hoping that maybe once she was out and I was done with my commitment at the tattoo shop, we could head back to Paris together, pick up where we'd left off.

Still, I couldn't complain. The time she spent at the facility was paying off. Slowly, but surely she was becoming my true Ree—the girl I'd seen glimpses of and fallen hard for. She'd always been there, but had too often been eclipsed by all-consuming pain. Now the sadness in her eyes was ebbing, giving way to strength and determination.

And happiness.

This last week, instead of being submerged in the darkness of the past and talking about the mindfuck that was her family, she'd focused on looking toward a brighter future. Her dream of discovering talent and covering the walls of her own gallery with art was no longer just a fantasy. She now saw it as a reality, a real possibility. And I was going to do whatever it took to help her realize it.

Running with Leo had become a morning ritual of sorts. It relieved some of my tension. Not to mention, it got me away from the constant orgy inside the house. It was as if every member of No Man's Land—save for Leo who had a girl back in L.A.—was trying to fuck someone out of their mind. Two or three times night.

It didn't help that rock stars apparently gave zero flying fucks about noise levels. "The louder, the better" was the motto around here. Listening to what I could only assume they'd call "research" for their *Nailed to the Wall* album was driving me nuts.

Not because I cared that they were screwing their way through all of Amsterdam. And not even because Synner kept sending half-naked chicks to my bed in search of something I had no intention of giving them. It was the knowledge that the only girl in the entire city I wanted was out of reach.

Today's three mile run had to hold me over just until tomorrow.

Tomorrow, when Ree returned to me.

Finally.

"Mind if I hit the shower first?" Leo asked as soon as we returned. "Indie is going to have my balls if I'm late to the studio again. She will literally chop them off, string them into a necklace, and wear them around her neck where Syn's currently hang."

"Thanks for the unnecessary visual," I said with a groan. "Yeah, go ahead. Defend your boys."

"Thanks, man. You're a nut-saver." He clapped me on the back as I headed over to the fridge in search of a bottle of water.

I made it halfway across the living room before a muffled shout from Dash's bedroom stopped me in my tracks.

"What the hell is wrong with you?!" The woman's voice was high-pitched and laced with a strong Irish accent. "Good lord. FINE! I'm getting out, you arse!"

His door burst open and a tall, curvy chick in her mid-twenties tornadoed through the living room. Long, auburn hair whirled about her as she grabbed her leather jacket and shoes, then slammed the front door.

Dash stumbled out of his room in just his black jeans—all six-feet three-inches of him looming in the doorway—looking like he'd just seen a ghost. "Fucking fuck!" He smashed the doorframe with his fist and stalked over to the kitchen.

Following closely behind, I said, "What the hell did you do to her?"

"Fuck, fuck, fuck..." He shook his head, and went straight for the coffee, the string of curses growing longer with each passing second.

"Dash...what did you do?"

He let out something that sounded like a half-groan, half-moan. "I crossed a boundary I shouldn't have."

"Her ass?" I raised my eyebrows and leaned against the fridge door.

"No," he said, gripping the kitchen counter, his eyes fixed on the coffee pot. "Her *hair*."

I reached over and poured him a cup because he clearly needed one and wasn't moving to do it himself. He just kept cursing and shaking his head as his knuckles turned whiter and whiter.

"Her hair? What the hell did you do to her hair

that had her running scared?"

"Her hair was fucking red." The words came out through clenched teeth.

"Jesus." I ran a hand over my face. "You're making absolutely no sense."

Dash shook his head. "I thought her fucking hair was brown," he said. "Last night at the club it looked dark brown. But this morning I woke up next to a redhead!" He lifted his head up. "FUUUUCK!"

"Okay," I said, frowning. "Sounds like an honest mistake." I'd had some unfortunate beer-goggle incidents when I'd been trying to fuck Ree out of my head. I was glad I'd been drunk enough to forget most as soon as they were over. "Not sure what you're getting so upset about. Shit happens, Dash."

"I don't make mistakes." His jaw tightened. "And I don't DO redheads!"

"Funny, I could've sworn you did anything and everything with a pulse." I laughed, relaxing a little. Though, the more I thought about it, I realized that in the two months I'd been with the band not a single redhead had come out of my brother's room. Dash shot me a look that could've cut through glass, so I raised my hands and backed off. "Okay, okay. No red-haired chicks. Got it." More seriously, I added, "So you didn't actually hurt her, right?"

"Of course not. I just told her to get the fuck out."

"Because of her hair." I started laughing again.

He nodded. "Yeah."

"Alright then," I said with a shrug. "I personally find your war on gingers baffling and *hairist* as shit, but at least we aren't going to have any trouble on our hands. Save for your poor girl's bruised ego."

"She's not MY girl." He growled the words as his fingers impulsively drifted to the little wren on his chest.

Interesting. "You know, if you have such a stick up your ass about redheads, maybe you shouldn't have let me add so much auburn to your wren tattoo. All those dark red feathers—"

"Shut it, Dare." His grip tightened around his coffee cup. "You may be blood, but do not go there."

VERY interesting.

Before either of us could say anything more, my phone buzzed, the caller ID lighting up with Rex's number.

Today was turning out to be full of surprises. "If you're calling to ask about Jasmine for the third time this week, she's safe and sound," I said as I picked up. "And still very married."

"Dare…" Rex's voice caused a chill to run down my spine.

There were only three reasons he would sound like that. Two of those were currently partying in Vienna. The other—my mom—I hadn't talked to for a week. Shit.

"What is it? What happened?"

"Your mom's counselor called." I could hear him sigh. "She's been skipping her meetings."

I ran a hand through my hair, at a loss for words. "Why?" was all I could manage. "Why now?" She had been doing SO well lately. She'd earned her one year sobriety chip just last month.

"Something has her spooked," he said.

Spooked? *Shit.* That could only mean—

Dash leaned in and mouthed, *What's wrong?*

I shook my head, worry taking hold, and turned on the speaker so Dash could hear.

"Rex?" I said. "What happened?"

"She got a call from Rykers."

All the air rushed out of my lungs. Dash white-knuckled the edge of the counter.

"When?" we both asked in unison. As if that REALLY mattered.

He had found her number. He had found her.

FUCK.

Rex didn't speak for what felt like an eternity. Finally, he said, "Two weeks ago. He said he was coming for her, that he was being released soon. She pleaded with me not to tell you, but I can't keep it from you now that she's missing meetings." Another few heartbeats of silence followed. "I'm sorry, Dare. This is my fault. I should be taking better care of her while you kids are away."

I shook my head. "Rex, it's enough that you flew to L.A. to be with her this summer so Dalia and Dax could travel and I could be here. The last thing you should be doing is blaming yourself. She's not your responsibility. She's mine."

And so was my father and his threat.

Dash bent down to the speaker and asked the one question I wasn't brave enough to ask. "Is Celia using again?"

"From what I can tell she's clean," Rex said, and I breathed a small sigh of relief. "I'm keeping a close eye on her and I'll drag her to those goddamn meetings if I have to. She's safe, Dare. I swear. I just thought you should know why she hasn't been herself lately. She's so afraid to tell you about Daren's call."

That name. That fucking name still haunted me to this day.

"Maybe I should come back," I said.

"No!" There was a sharp edge in Rex's voice. "You need to live YOUR life. *For once.* Your mom will be fine."

"Rex—"

"No, Dare. Listen to me. You stay where you are. If you show up here all of a sudden, that's just going to spook her more."

I nodded, torn. For the moment, he was probably right. If she was already scared, it could send her over the edge, and I really didn't want to be the cause of her falling off the wagon again.

"Okay," I said. "I'll stay. But you call me the minute you hear anything at all. Promise me that, Rex."

"Of course. If anything changes, I'll call."

As soon as Rex hung up, Dash began pacing the room.

"I'll call my mom and see if he's been in touch," he said, running his fingers through his hair. "We don't know if it's really him yet."

My head pounded. "Sure we do, Dash. My mom doesn't have that many admirers from Rykers."

"At least we know he's still incarcerated, right?" I was pretty sure Dash had meant that to sound reassuring. Except his words had the opposite effect.

"Yeah," I said with a shrug. "For now."

Ree had warned me that her father had the power to reduce my dad's sentence. She had also told me what she'd said to the reporters back in the Galerie Yves Robert. The message she'd had for her parents. If the mayor saw me as the reason she was dissing Harvard and the McKinley name...*shit*.

"Maybe it's nothing," Dash said.

Where the hell did his optimism come from? Did it have something to do with the fact that Dash had never crossed our father the way that I had? That fucker had never had it as bad for anyone as he'd had it for me. His name on my birth certificate was like a target on my back.

"Maybe I need to go back home," I said, placing my head in my hands.

"When I got out of rehab," Dash said, quietly, "I had someone who helped me through it all, and I never would have made it to sobriety without her. But if she hadn't been there for me at that time..."

His voice trailed off and I lifted my head to look at him. He had this far-off look in his eyes— a painful mixture of sweetness and sorrow on his face.

I immediately knew what I needed to do, what I *wanted* to do.

For the moment, I needed to put this out of my mind and focus on Ree. Right now, there was nothing in the world I wanted more than to help her win this fight. I had to do everything in my power to ensure her happiness. That also meant not telling her about my parents. If she got even one whiff of the potential threat—especially if it was brought on by her father—it could send her running for the pills again.

I would just have to take things one day at a time and trust that everything would work out. *For once.*

Having lived in the middle of a shitstorm for so long, I'd taken the relative quiet of the last few years to be a deserved respite. Having Ree in my life had to be my reward for all the hurt I'd survived growing up.

I just had to hope this wasn't the calm before the real storm.

fourteen
Reagan

"Ready?" Dare squeezed my hand and smiled as we stood on the doorstep of Dash's place.

Yeah, the former scene of my worst walk of shame ever. Talk about your first test straight out of rehab. My heart was pounding, my palms sweating, and I felt like I couldn't get any oxygen into my lungs.

I started shaking my head. "I don't know about this, Dare."

The people inside were foreign to me. Not to mention, the last time they'd seen me had not been my most shining moment, to say the least. I had a vague recollection of insulting some girl with blue hair before realizing Dare was there, and then hanging my head as Dash had walked me out. Sure, the eldest Wilde had been incredibly kind, but he had to think the worst of me. Anyone would.

God, I wished I had some pills to settle my nerves.

Shit.

I couldn't think like that. I had to be able to do it on my own, to live life without help. I'd already faced much worse in my past. I had to be able to handle *this* with my head held high.

"Ree." Dare's lips were pressed against my ear, his warm breath shivering me. "They're not going to judge you. Some of them have been where you are—Dash has, for one." I pulled back from him so I could see his eyes. Dash had been in rehab? Somehow, I could breathe a little easier knowing that. "They don't know you. You have a clean slate with them. I promise you have nothing to worry about."

I nodded, took a breath, and then tried to smile.

"Think about them like they're your new therapy group," he said. "Out of one rehab program and into—"

"No man's land?" I said, a genuine smile blooming. "That doesn't sound dangerous at all."

Dare laughed, shaking his head. "No, it doesn't." Then he reached over and brushed his thumb across my cheek. "I'm here. Okay?"

Leaning into his hand, I sighed. "Yeah," I said, kissing his palm. "I can do this."

"I know."

No one had ever believed in me before, and his words filled me with strength.

His strength. My strength. *Our* strength.

"So…are you ready?" he asked, gently nudging my shoulder.

Not really, but I was never fully going to be. Might as well make this first step.

I nodded. "Ready as I'll ever be. Let's go."

He opened the door, and I followed him inside.

"—don't understand why we can't at least have beer here," a male voice was saying. "And why aren't there any women?"

There was a loud smack and the guy said "OW! Jesus, Indie, that fucking hurt!"

The band members were assembled around the dining room table. All four of them, save for Dash.

Food was set out along the breakfast bar and the table as if they were having a party, and there were a couple of bottles of soda, seltzer, and juice. But not a drop of alcohol to be seen.

Because of me. No. FOR me.

I wasn't sure whether to feel touched at the gesture or guilty that they were being denied. A little bit of both settled over me.

"And what am *I*, Hawke?" The blue-haired girl glared at a tall guy with messy black hair and tribal tattoos winding around both arms.

"A fucking banshee," another guy said, and the girl reached over and smacked him on the back of his dirty blond head. "Bloody hell, Blue. No matter how much you wish I was, I'm not your boy toy anymore."

Synner. I bit back a smile.

A dark-skinned guy with short hair grabbed a handful of chips. "Hawke meant *real women*, Indie. Not you."

Indie's eyes widened into huge blue saucers. She planted her hands on her hips, and I could practically see steam coming out of her ears. "I'm not a REAL WOMAN, Leo?"

He glared at her. "It's *Lynx*, Banshee. And I'm not sure...Synner? You're the only one who's had her. Is she a real woman?"

"She sure screamed like one." Synner ducked when Indie swung at his head again. "Aw, come on, Blue," he said, laughing as he dodged every one of her blows. "It's thanks to me that you can reach all those high notes now."

"Well, in THAT case..." Hawke grabbed Indie, threw her over his shoulder and started carrying her toward what I could only assume was his bedroom.

"Put me down this minute, Hawke, or I swear you'll NEVER have children!"

Hawke laughed as she pounded her fists into his back, then gently set her back on the floor. As soon as her feet hit the ground, she kneed him in the groin. Then she spun around, her blue hair flying as she stalked away, while Synner and Leo howled at Hawke doubled over in pain.

As soon as Indie saw Dare and me standing in the doorway, she stopped. Then she glanced back at the guys in the kitchen, rolled her eyes, and with a resigned sigh said, "Welcome to the island of horny, immature misfit toys, Ree."

Dash showed up a little while later with several girls in tow. Hawke, Leo, and Synner immediately dropped the juvenile delinquents act and morphed into slick rock stars. I couldn't help but laugh as I watched them put well-practiced moves on the groupies.

Indie, who'd claimed me since I was apparently "the only other voice of reason in this male-infested flat," shook her head.

"If those women only knew what these children I live with were REALLY like," she said as the groupies swooned over her bandmates, "they'd run screaming out of here." She eyed them from where we sat on the couch. "That is, if they had any sense, and from the way they're drooling over the guys, they clearly don't."

Thirty minutes with the band, and I was already falling a little bit in love with everyone. I was also feeling so incredibly welcomed amidst their beautiful mayhem.

Most importantly, I was not craving my pills.

It was both a strange and liberating feeling.

At least until Sia strutted in, and it felt like the shadow of a storm cloud suddenly fell over me.

Dare's eyebrows shot up at the sight of her, and he glanced over at me from where he stood in the kitchen with Dash. He'd stayed by my side until Indie had taken over—almost like they were tag-teaming me—but then he'd gone to get something to drink and hadn't come back yet. He and Dash were talking quietly—and about something serious from the tense expressions on their faces. But even so, every few minutes I felt Dare's eyes on me, warming me, checking in as he made sure I was okay.

And I was. I was more than okay.

Well, I had been. As soon Sia stepped into the room, her words echoed in my head. *People don't change...especially not addicts.*

But I had. My chin lifted a little. I *was* changing.

So why did my fingers itch for my little bottle as soon as I saw her?

I excused myself from Indie and walked down the hall to the bathroom. Closing the door behind me, I felt like I was shutting out the world, keeping myself safe.

But then I saw the medicine cabinet.

My feet brought me to it before my mind could even register what was happening. I stared at my reflection without really seeing myself, too busy wondering what treasures were on the little shelves behind the mirror. Gripping the sink, I gazed into my own eyes—bright, clear, focused. I was in total control of myself, and I liked that feeling. More than I thought I would. Now that I had finally achieved it, there was no way in hell I would give it up so easily.

The pills were calling to me, but I wasn't going to listen. Not this time. Not ever again.

Hopefully.

Defiantly, I glared at the cabinet, but instead of opening it, I leaned over the sink and splashed water on my face.

I could do this. I *would* do this. I wasn't ready to lose it on my first day out. Picturing Dare's face filled with pride and love gave me an extra jolt of strength.

When I opened the bathroom door, Sia was waiting in the hallway, her arms crossed, her eyes narrowed as if I was some kind of prey.

"How are you doing, hun?" She crooned, her voice syrupy sweet. Her eyebrows were drawn up together in the middle of her forehead in mock concern. The fake smile that lifted her bright red lips made my stomach turn.

Yeah, some people never change. She was still a stone-cold bitch.

"I'm fine," I said, and tried to brush past her, but she shot out an arm and snaked it around my shoulders, turning me toward the back of the house, away from the others.

Then she lowered her voice to a dark whisper. "I'm sure you are," she said. "And I know how hard it can be, so I brought you this. Just in case."

She pulled her hand out of her pocket and opened her palm to reveal a little bottle.

Of pills.

Oh, god.

"You know you're going to need them sometime," Sia said.

My gaze was glued to the bottle, and my body began to shake. Out of the corner of my eye I could see her shit-eating grin growing wider.

Fucking hell. I needed to get hold of myself. A firm grip on reality.

I shook my head and tried to shut my eyes so I could focus on something else, but I couldn't peel my eyes from the bottle.

"I don't want it," I said, more to convince myself than her.

"Of *course* you don't." She let out a tiny laugh. "But you'll need it. You know that, right?"

The pills in the bottle called to me, singing a sweet siren song only I could hear. And they really needed to shut the fuck up right now.

I grabbed the bottle out of Sia's hand and strode back into the bathroom. She followed me, looking like she was about to crow. Her face filled with sickening glee as I twisted the lid off and peered inside.

"It's hard coming back to the real world," she said with pretend care in her voice. "These'll help take the edge off." She grabbed the glass from the edge of the sink and turned on the faucet as I lifted the lid of the toilet, tipped the bottle, and watched the pills tumble into the water.

Sia's face froze when she turned to hand me the water.

I glared at her even as my hands still shook. "I'm sure Dare is wondering where I am," I said, then pushed past her and headed toward the front of the house.

"He needs someone like me, bitch. Someone stable." Her voice halted me, and I turned to face her again. She'd come back out into the hallway, the filled glass still in her hand. "We have a history together. You have no place in his life."

Anger flushed hot on my face. "That's not what he says."

"We fucked. Did he tell you that?"

Her words shivered into my skin like ice shards, and I couldn't help wonder, *When? When had they fucked? When he came to Amsterdam?*

And did it matter even if they had? Because I knew he'd been mine since the day I said I'd go to rehab. I knew it in my soul. That was all that really mattered in the end.

"We were made for each other. And you?" She

stalked up to me, practically pressing her nose into mine as her dark eyes tried to burn a hole through me. "You were made for—"

"Me," Dare said from behind me. Sia's head whipped up as she gasped. He slipped his arms around my waist, pulling me tight against him. "Ree was made for me."

I closed my eyes and leaned into the wall of hard muscle behind me. Threading my fingers through his, I felt my body relax as it filled up with his love and his warmth.

"Time for you to go, Sia." Dare's voice was dangerously low, and I opened my eyes to see the hurt and anger flashing across Sia's face. "You're not welcome here if you're going to talk to Ree like that."

Sia glared at me, then pushed past us, hurrying down the hall. I turned in Dare's arms, slid my hands up his chest and locked them tightly around his neck. Pulling his face down to mine, I melded against his body and kissed him with everything I was feeling in that moment.

"You okay?" he said when we parted, his eyes searching my face.

"I'm better than that." Grinning, I took his hand and led him back out to the living room, to everyone I wanted to be with.

I was glad Sia was gone, but I was also strangely glad she'd come. Filled with a selfish need to destroy me, she had been my first true test. And I'd passed. I hadn't kept the bottle.

This night no longer felt like a single step. It was bounding leap.

I was finally starting to rise up from the ashes.

fifteen
Reagan

"Breathe, Ree," Dare's voice was the only thing still anchoring me to this world. And even his low, commanding tone seemed miles away.

"*Mmmhmm…*" I felt his black-gloved hands on my hips, but I didn't chance a peek at what they were doing.

"Relax," he said, shaking me slightly as he pressed down into my skin. "You're going to pass out if you keep holding your breath."

I was pretty damn sure I would pass out regardless.

It was Sunday afternoon, and he had suggested getting started on my tattoo while the shop was closed for the day. So, here I was, lying on my side across his table, peach crochet top up, white denim shorts shimmied down my hips.

All alone. With Dare. And needles.

Thoughts of both made my head spin. If I lost consciousness, it could be from either fear or arousal. Most likely, a combination of the two.

Which was slightly twisted, but we were going on fifteen days of barely any physical contact, and even though I'd been discharged from Feniks yesterday, between the party that went on until the early morning hours and the constant presence of the band members, the most Dare and I had been able to squeeze in was just a handful of kisses.

I wanted, craved, NEEDED my fix. All of him.

My heart hurt. Other parts of me ached for him.

If there was anything I'd learned in rehab, it was that pills were easier to resist than Dare.

I squealed when I felt something cold press into my side, and Dare laughed. "Just the stencil." He ran the back of his hand over my cheek, slowly trailing his knuckles down my neck and over my shoulder. "The needles are still safely packed away. I'm not going to hurt you."

"*Yet.*" I didn't have many fears, but my phobia of needles went hand-in-hand with my fear of dark, underground spaces. One day soon, I would have the courage to tell Dare the full story. Every. Shameful. Detail. Today, though, I just wanted my phoenix.

"I promise to make every bit of pain worth your while." A wickedly delicious grin flashed across his lips, making my heart hammer so loud I was certain he could hear every beat. "Trust me.

You're in good hands."

"I know." I pressed my lips together and nodded. "I don't doubt that." I just wished those hands were doing other things right now instead of preparing to puncture my skin.

But Dare seemed to be in his zone where nothing but art existed. Considering I was going to have his work permanently engraved on my body, I supposed that was a good thing.

Still, a greedy—and extremely horny—part of me couldn't get over the effect of his proximity. My mind was filled with fantasies of him mounting me on this table right now, spreading my legs wide so he could push himself so deeply into me that we became one.

At the thought, my thighs parted, and a small moan slipped past my lips. I heard Dare suck in a sharp breath. A quick glance up at his face revealed eyes as dark as sin, trained directly on the spot between my legs that throbbed with need for him. My pulse accelerated as I felt—yes, physically *felt*—him devouring me in his mind.

Our last time had been two weeks ago when he had "painted" me with his tongue. His fingers had felt so good gliding over every inch of my skin, his mouth so hot and greedy as he sucked on my clit. This time, I gritted my teeth to keep the moan from escaping.

Too late.

Pulling his gaze away, Dare bent his head to mine and grazed my ear with his lips. "You can't keep making those sweet, little sounds while I'm working," he said. "The quickest way to get me to fuck up the tattoo is to make me think about fucking you here on this table. Behave, Princess."

"Easier said than done." My cheeks burned. Other parts of me were just as affected by the lust in his eyes and the filth of his words. Clearly, he wasn't as far gone into the art zone as I had thought.

"So, this isn't all bad, huh?" He smirked and pressed his mouth to my forehead. How could such a quick kiss make my entire world spin? "I just have to make sure the stencil is locked in and then we'll break so you can take a look," he said. "Find something…*safe*…to focus on for the next twenty seconds."

With Dare's hands still on me, safe was out of the question. But I focused on something that had been weighing on me for the past few days. A topic I'd been avoiding bringing up since it could mean some time apart. But I had to get it over with. Sooner, rather than later.

"Sabine called while I was at the center." I bit my lip and took a deep breath. "She offered me a position as curator of an upcoming worldwide exhibition. Full control of the artists. Well paid."

Dare let out a low whistle. "That lady never

ceases to amaze me."

I nodded my agreement. "She's my fairy godmother," I said, becoming more animated about the idea of working, of having a REAL life finally. "It's the opportunity of a lifetime."

"Sounds great. When do you start?"

"Two weeks." I cleared my throat. "In Paris."

His shoulders tensed, but he didn't say anything except a quick, "Huh."

I had it all planned out. I'd even looked into support groups in the area that I could attend. One of Gino's associates had agreed to take me on for my weekly counseling sessions. The only thing missing was…Dare.

"I was wondering," I said, suddenly filled with more fear than any needle could inspire, "would you by any chance want to…?"

Oh, god. Why were my hands shaking? It wasn't like I was fucking proposing.

I was just asking him to follow me to another country. On many levels, that was probably a more intimate request than marriage. Especially considering everything we had been through in the past few months. But I had to try. I had to show him I was done running. Dare needed to know I wanted to be with him, that I wanted to do this together.

For real. Forever.

The question was, would he?

"I know this is new for both of us, but now that I've finally found you I don't want to let you go," I said. "*Ever.* I can't live through losing you again." My voice shook; the thought was too much. "So, I wanted to ask if you'd come with me."

His gaze lifted to mine, his eyes widening slightly.

Shit. What did that mean?

"It's only for two months," I was now talking a mile a minute, "and I know if I don't take this job I would be making a mistake, but at the same time being with you—"

"Yes."

"Yes?" Just like that? I couldn't breathe—all my dreams were coming together at once. He seriously just said *yes*.

"I've still got my place in Paris," he said. "We can stay there. Give this a real go. I was actually thinking we might go back. I miss my work. My real work. Tattooing isn't enough." Pinning me with that sexy, dark gaze, he added, "And spending the next two months without you isn't an option. Not now when you're finally, wholly mine."

My jaw hung open. "You want to *live* with me?"

He laughed. "Sure. Or you can live across the hall again. But that prick Archer isn't welcome anywhere near the apartment building."

"Neither is Giselle."

His eyebrows knitted together. "Who?"

The fact that he'd forgotten the French beauty so soon made me glow.

Good freaking riddance.

"I'm committed to Jasmine and the shop for another month," he said. "So you'll have to go ahead without me, but I'll be right behind you." His mouth tightened, the muscles of his jaw rippling tensely. "I hate the idea of you being there all alone for two weeks."

"I'm a big girl. I'll be living my dream and waiting for the guy I love." Then I realized what his strained expression meant. "And I'll be staying away from the party scene."

"What about the dark?"

"I can handle the dark." The darkness was still there, waiting to consume me. But now I had more tools and support to fight it. "As long as you're mine, I can handle anything." My chest filled with warmth. So much warmth that I felt as if I'd stepped into an alternate reality where things actually worked out in my favor. "We can do this, Dare. I know we can."

We'd survived three years. And lived through twenty-eight days. We could handle two weeks.

We would be happy. Finally.

He removed his gloves and gently nudged my shoulder. "Ready to see what your phoenix will look like?"

"Hell yeah," I said as he helped me off the padded table and guided me to a full-length mirror in the corner.

He stood behind me, his fingers closed around mine, keeping my bunched up shirt in place while he turned me to the side. "What do you think?"

"Oh, god...." My heart caught in my throat. There was no single word to describe the outline of the magnificent creature that would soon be a permanent part of my body. She was even better than the image he had painted on me all those years ago.

"You won't have the full picture until I start tattooing and put in all the shading and the golds and reds, but—"

"She's perfect, Dare. MORE than perfect." The phoenix stretched across my right side, her fiery wings licking my back, her tail curved slightly down my hip. She was feminine, majestic, regal. More powerful than anything I'd ever seen. "She's not even inked on my skin yet, but she makes me feel so...*alive*."

I pulled my shirt over my head and let it fall to the floor, moving my loose braid over my shoulder in the process. "I want to see what they look like together," I said, tugging at the hem of his black tee. "Please."

His eyes flitted to the thin, slightly see-through

lace of my bra before he bowed his head and grabbed the material at the back of his neck, pulling the t-shirt off to expose his tattoo.

It was now my turn to stare. Even though my fingers and lips knew every inch of hard muscle and smooth, tanned skin, I could never get enough. Dare was all sharp edges and sculpted curves—so damn edible, and he somehow managed to look MORE delicious every time I saw him.

The sight of his tight pecs and carved abs caused heat to spread throughout me. My heart fluttered and my knees wobbled. Apparently I turned into a lust-filled maniac in his presence.

This is your brain on drugs? Screw that. *This is your brain on Dare.*

Hello, dopamine overload. Goodbye, rational thought.

I refused to peek at the triangle of muscle protruding from the waist of his jeans, in fear I'd probably end up on my knees, tearing at his fly with my teeth. Instead, I made my way up his body—over the paintbrush tattoo on the inside of his forearm, and followed the snake winding around his bicep to the black phoenix on his shoulder.

Pressing my back into him, I rose up on my tiptoes and wrapped my arms around his neck, bringing our two birds as close as possible. The image in the mirror took my breath away.

Our two birds signified the same rebirth—each of us rebuilding our lives, reclaiming ourselves, becoming who we wanted to be, not who we'd been sentenced to be by our fathers.

Dare really was the light in my darkness. I'd always known it. And now everyone else would, too. Even my parents, if I ever saw them again.

"You like?" he asked.

"I love," I said, my entire soul humming. And I laughed—it bubbled up in my chest, spilling over into the room—because looking at myself in the mirror right now I felt genuinely beautiful for the first time in my life. I felt like ME for the first time. Reagan—the cold, unhappy bitch who used to mock me, telling me I would never be good enough for anything—was gone. In her place was Ree.

Me.

"Thank you, Dare."

His reflection arched an eyebrow at me. "For what?"

For saving my life. "The tattoo," I said.

He shook his head and pressed a devilish smile into my shoulder. "I haven't even started inking yet. If you're into premature appreciation, maybe you should first thank me for something else." A sly grin crossed his face as he hooked his fingers into the back of my shorts. "Before I start tattooing, I need to see what you'll look like the next time I paint you," he said, slowly sliding them past my hips and over the curve of my butt. "I want you down to just your phoenix."

An excited shudder ran up my spine as the cool air in the room hit my bare skin. The ache between my legs grew even stronger when he guided the shorts down to the floor. His palms trailed back up my legs, insatiable fingers gliding over my skin, sending my senses spinning.

"Wow, if I'd known I'd get this kind of treatment at a tattoo parlor, I would have done this a long time ago. Though you better not do this with all your clients."

"Nah." His chest vibrated with laughter. "I reserve my best work only for the ones I love," he said. Then he ran one hand up the back of my leg and squeezed my ass. The humor in his eyes was overtaken by something darker and headier. "And those I care about marking as mine."

The realization that he truly was about to permanently brand me with his art—and, in turn, HIMSELF—hit me hard. My body responded instantly, the tingling in my core spreading out into my whole system, making my heart race. I was so turned on my senses felt a hundred times stronger and more powerful. I could practically taste, feel, and hear the pleasure that he was promising in just that single look.

My nipples hardened behind the barely-there material covering them, once again drawing Dare's attention to my breasts. He brushed his fingers across the fabric, sending jolts of pleasure through me, then claimed one, squeezing lightly and pulling it toward his mouth so he could wrap his lips around the pink peak. The combination of his warm, wet tongue and the soft tickle of lace he licked me through just about undid me.

My legs gave out, and I lost my balance, but he caught me...by the waistband of my thong, making the fabric slide across my swollen clit. He positioned me so that I was standing directly in front of him, my body on display in the mirror for him. Still holding onto my panties, he unclasped my bra with one hand, freeing me from its constraints.

"So beautiful," he whispered in my ear. Cupping my breast with one hand, he pulled back on my thong with the other, bringing me deeper into him, rubbing my clit again. Then he released the pressure. Pull, release, pull, release. With the fabric grazing my throbbing clit every time, my hips started to rock with his motions as I moaned. "Do you see how fucking beautiful you are, Ree?"

I blushed at the image in front of me—messy braid, wide eyes, parted pink lips, quivering legs. I looked like I was possessed. Possessed by happiness and Dare. And probably also on the verge of orgasm if he kept moving my thong like that.

He wrapped my braid around his fingers and gently tugged my head back, claiming my mouth as his lips and tongue scattered my thoughts. Between his ownership of my lips, the firm grip on my hair, and his possessive claim over my thong, I was his. Completely and entirely his.

"Just a little pre-tat relaxation technique," he said, pulling away, but not entirely breaking contact.

"Earning my trust, Wilde?"

"Just one of the many things I plan to acquire by this session's end." His lips burned kisses into my jaw and neck, latching on my wild pulse as he released my braid and slid his hand down my stomach to my front. His fingers ventured under the lace to cup my heat, and a loud groan thundered through him as he slid one finger inside me. "Fuck, you feel incredible."

Skilled fingers skimmed my clit, flicking and massaging while his other hand continued to tug on my thong. The erotic blend of his fingers and the taut material sweeping over my folds made my head spin in ways I didn't think was humanly possible. Energy was building up in my core, the throb between my legs was growing and growing, taking me higher and higher.

I was about to come. And probably also die.

"Hands on the mirror." I heard Dare's whisper in my ear, his voice hoarse with arousal. "Don't pass out on me, Ree. This is supposed to be the fun part."

Using the glassy surface for support, I rocked my hips back into him, giving him complete access, urging him to delve deeper, harder, faster, moving to the rhythm he set. His gaze firmly locked onto mine as I grinded against the rock-hard bulge in his jeans until we were both moaning.

Little jolts of electricity flowed through my veins and the throbbing between my thighs had me begging for release. The tingling intensified and I was already calling out his name, the pressure inside me barreling full speed ahead toward a cosmic blast when—

He stopped.

Completely. Fucking. Stopped.

A small whimper of protest escaped my lips, but Dare quickly extinguished it with his kiss. Closing my eyes, I lost myself in the sensation of his tongue, then moaned as I felt him rip off my thong.

Still, his fingers never returned to *that* spot. The one place that really, REALLY needed him right now.

Instead, he released me and took a step back, nodding at the tattoo table. "Get on." His breaths were controlled while mine were nothing more than quick, raspy pants. His eyes were so perilous yet alluring, and I had no idea what he was going to do.

All I could think was that he was planning something big. Like him—deep inside me.

Or maybe this was about something small, but terrifying. Like a needle.

God. The unknown was both scary and hot as hell.

I walked over the table, pausing at its side, running my hand over the clean sheet Dare had draped over it for me. "How do you want me?"

He inhaled sharply and cursed under his breath. "How many times did you ask me that exact question in Paris while I painted you? How many times did I have to grit my teeth and stop myself from describing in detail every position I wanted to take you in just because you weren't mine?"

The sensual ache in my body returned at those words, pleading to be satiated. "Well, I am yours now." I leaned against the edge of the table, offering myself up to him. "So…take me. Please, *please* take me."

His eyes glided over my exposed body, pausing at the peaks of my nipples before dipping to the stencil on my skin, and traveling even farther south. "Lie on your back," he said.

When I did, he wrapped his fingers around my wrists. Pulling them up above my head, he gently guided my hands to the sides of the table. "Hold on tight. Don't let go," he said, then moved back down, hovering over me as he paused at my lips. "And don't you dare move."

Oh, god.

He adjusted the table, and leaned over his equipment where the sterilized needle was ready and waiting in the machine. Every muscle in my body went rigid, and my heart attempted to leap out of my chest when he picked up his gloves.

Shit, shit, shit.

My gasp caught his attention. "Ree, look at me," he said, claiming my chin between his fingers and pressing his forehead to mine. "I'm not going to hurt you. Do you trust me?"

"Yes." I had to show him I was strong, that I was worthy of this beautiful phoenix's power.

"Good." He seized my lower lip between his teeth. "Because what I'm about to do breaks the rules of both tattooing *and* fucking."

"First rehab, now tattoo parlor. You're breaking all kinds of rules."

"You only have yourself to thank for that," he said.

I laughed, feeling the tension melt away as a different kind of thrill ran through me. "So...we're starting with the outline?"

He nodded. "I'm going to do a quick test run first. Make sure you can handle it."

I squeezed my thighs together, simultaneously turned on and scared. I expected Dare to start the machine, but instead he kissed his way from my lips, down my neck to my chest. He pulled one nipple into his mouth, sucking and nipping at it, before moving to the other to do the same. He then kissed his way down my stomach until his lips were nibbling right above my core, and I was already rocking to the rhythm of my pulsing sweet spot.

When he parted my thighs and brought his mouth right back to where I needed him so badly, the urge to grab his hair trumped his orders to keep still. His tongue lapped at my folds, swirled around my clit, teasing, taunting. My hips bucked under the pressure of his mouth, and my fingers wrapped around his short, dark locks.

"You're cheating." His voice hummed against me in low warning.

My body quivered under his touch as I panted in reply. "And you're playing dirty."

I could've sworn I felt him smile. "Tell me you don't love it," he said.

Oh, god, I fucking loved each lick and every nibble. My response came in the form of a loud moan.

"Good." He spread my knees wider and thrust his tongue deeper. "Now, hands on the table, Ree."

I gripped the table again, allowing him free reign. His tongue drove me wild, and my body was already wound so tight from what he'd done to me by the mirror that my climax approached quickly and forcefully. Once again, just as I was about to launch off the edge and burst apart, he pulled away, leaving me aching in pleasure-infused agony.

FUCK. ME.

"*Please…*"

He licked his lips and grinned. "Not yet. We have a long session ahead of us."

A little part of me wanted to scream in frustration, but a much bigger piece was excited as hell by the idea of more Dare, more…*this*.

"I need you on your side. And you're going to have to be very still for this part." He put on his gloves, then massaged cool ointment over the stenciled area of my skin, and I immediately knew what was coming next.

The pain part of *pleasure and pain.*

The first few stings of the needle caused me to bite down on my lip, but the next few weren't so bad. Soon, all I was focusing on was the soft hum of the machine and the way Dare's eyes seemed to be worshiping each line and every stroke he made. Whenever he paused to wipe, the corners of his lips lifted into a reassuring smile that seemed to be aimed straight at my heart.

With the outline of the wings done, he shifted back into *pleasure* mode, putting down the gun to lavish attention on my mouth, nipples, and stomach, finally ending up back between my legs, teasing me hard and fast with his tongue and fingers before pulling away yet again to return to the phoenix's body.

By the time the outline was completed, I was a complete mess. Not due to the discomfort, but because of the desperate need for release that was driving me to the edge. I'd barely felt any pain while he tattooed, but every time he kissed, licked, and touched me, a raw unfulfilled ache tore through my insides. Sprawled on the table with my hands above my head, I had been completely at his mercy, and my body was starting to rebel. I was so tightly wound and so incredibly turned on, I felt like a single gust of air could be the trigger that pushed me over the edge.

"You did amazing," he whispered on a kiss. "We're done for now. I'll finish the rest next time."

I looked up at him with a wide, excited grin. "Do I get my reward?" Dare had delivered on his promise to take good care of me. Now I just hoped he'd finish the damn job, before I was forced to take matters into my own hands.

His shoulders shook with laughter. "You make it sound like you were the only one being tortured here. Try keeping your hand steady while tattooing a sexy, naked chick that keeps moaning your name over and over again as you work." He finished wrapping my tattoo, then bent his head and grazed his teeth over my collarbone. "We *both* get our reward," he said, his eyes full of fire. "Right fucking now."

NOW. That three-letter word had never sounded so sweet.

He moved to the foot of the table, pulling my ass all the way to the edge, spreading my legs so that they were wrapped around his hips. My arms still above my head, his gaze heated my skin as it raked over me, all the way from my mouth down to my throbbing core. He followed with his touch, running two fingers over my lips all the way down to heat deep inside my core.

"Please, Dare...I can't wait anymore."

My body shuddered and I let out an audible sigh of relief when I heard him unzip his jeans. Then he was pushing inside me, groaning and thrusting so deep, the answer to all my dirty fantasies and horny prayers.

I watched every muscle in his body tighten as he drove into me, his chiseled face an erotic portrait of arousal and need. One of his hands teased my nipples as the fingers of the other drifted up and down my thighs, first gentle, then growing in greed as his hips began to move faster and harder.

Looking down at me with his stormy gaze, he hooked his arms around my legs and lifted them up so they were resting against his shoulders, shooting me a satisfied grin when I cried out, knowing exactly how far into me that maneuver had brought him. I felt every long, hard inch fill me, stretch me, own me as he moved with powerful, piercing strokes.

The force of limitless delayed climaxes was locked within me, vibrating deep in my core, begging to be released. I was no longer teetering on the edge of some tall cliff...I was floating in space in a whole other universe, needing Dare to show me the way home.

His thumb touched down on my clit at the same time as he drove inside me, detonating the first quake. With every intense thrust, he set off a new wave of pleasure, each spasm taking me higher than the previous one. Arching my spine, my eyes rolling to the back of my head, I cried out his name through ragged breaths, experiencing what I could only describe as the best and longest orgasm of my life. Or rather, *orgasms*. It was impossible to tell when one ended and the next one began.

Just when I thought I'd died and gone to some kinky version of heaven, Dare leaned forward and slammed into me again, his eyes meeting mine as another toe-curling burst of delirium surged through me. I cried out his name, and he responded by groaning mine as his own release quaked his body.

He collapsed on top of me, careful to protect my bandaged side as he pressed his lips to mine, parting them with his tongue, and indulging in a long, leisurely taste of me. His kiss spread fire through my veins, reaching a place even deeper than the one he'd just come from.

"How do you feel?" he asked, glancing down at my covered tattoo.

"Free." I smiled into his mouth. "Happy." Excited to be on a path that finally seemed to be going in the right direction.

Ecstatic to be walking it with Dare.

sixteen
Reagan

"REE! You're here!" That familiar shriek only belonged to one Wilde. My body flooded with warmth at the sound of her voice. "Oh, hey, Dare."

"Dalia," Dare said without turning around, his attention focused entirely on my tattoo as he shaded the wings over my ribs. "So great to see that I'm just a postscript."

But he smiled as he said it. I knew how much he loved his siblings, and the fact that they'd taken me in, accepted me as one of their own meant a lot to him. He'd had enough crap in his family life, so any discord between me and them would not have gone over well. Honestly, it would've probably destroyed us long ago.

"Wow!" Dalia bent over Dare's arm to examine my ink. "The phoenix looks gorgeous on you. You're like a fiery, golden goddess, Ree."

"Holy crap. A half-NAKED goddess!" I didn't

even have to look to know where Dax's gaze was glued. I immediately pulled my shirt down a little. "Damn, don't shy away on my account, babe." He was practically panting. "I'm a big fan of Dare's nude work. In fact, I enjoy dabbling in some of my own. You wanna see?"

"Tell you what," I said with a teasing laugh, "if I ever stop being a fan of your brother's work, you'll be the first one I call."

"I'm the one with the gun in my hand, you know that, right?" Dare bent down to claim my bottom lip between his teeth. "You better watch what you say, Princess."

"Or what?" I let out a little squeal when he bit down. "Is that all you've got, Wilde?" There was a challenge in my voice. "Just empty threats and a few little nibbles?"

Lowering his lips to my ear, he said, "I *dare* you to leave me. See how far you get before I drag you back here and make you grip that table. Just like last week. Except my *nibbles* won't be so gentle, this time." He pulled back and pinned me with his gaze as we shared a heated look.

I felt my cheeks redden as my imagination went a little wild with the possibilities—things that were way too inappropriate to even THINK about with his sister and brother in the room.

Dalia giggled. "Look at you two. Such sweet lovebirds! No, wait. *Love-phoenixes.*"

Good thing Dalia couldn't see just how very *un*-sweet my thoughts were about Dare. And from the wicked grin on his face, his own were just as filthy.

Dare straightened up and looked over his shoulder at his siblings. "Take two steps back, Terrors," he said. "You're blocking my light."

I arched an eyebrow at him. "Terrors?"

Dalia rolled her eyes and Dax winked. I had no doubt he'd earned that nickname over and over again. And not just from Dare.

"Terrors," Dare said. "Ever since they crayoned my first sketchbook when they were five years old."

"Don't you think that's gotten a little old by now?" Dalia said, sinking her weight into one hip.

Dare nodded his chin at Dax. "Take a look at your twin right now ogling my girlfriend and you tell me if it's not well-deserved."

Dalia was popping Dax's arm even before she turned to him.

"What?" he said, a huge grin splitting his face. "I'm just fantasizing about how I can get a partially naked chick to let me draw all over her. Or better yet, a FULLY naked chick."

"GOD." Dalia groaned. "Do you actually hear the things that come out of your mouth?"

I bit back a smile and turned to Dalia. "Did you two just get in?"

"Yup. About an hour ago." She sank into an empty chair in the corner of the room and let out an exhausted sigh. "We dropped off our loot from Germany and Austria at Dash's, and booked it over here to see you guys right away."

"Just in time for the concert tonight," Dare said, turning off the machine and wiping down my skin.

"And all the GROUPIES," Dax said.

Dalia shook her head at her brother. "You know they're only interested in the hot band members, right?"

"What about the guitarist's hot younger brother?" Dax asked, wiggling his eyebrows.

"Nah." She dismissed him with a wave of her hand, her multi-colored nails making a rainbow in front of her face. "Dare's already taken," she said. "They don't stand a chance with him."

Dare threw his head back and laughed while Dax stared at Dalia with his mouth hanging open. I couldn't help but laugh with them, reveling in their warmth and love as I filled up on this amazing sense of belonging.

"Brilliant!" Synner said, sitting next to Dalia at the restaurant that night, surprisingly without a groupie by his side. A huge grin lit his face as he raised his glass. "A fucking brilliant concert tonight."

No Man's Land was glowing like the bright stars they were. The whole lot of them. Indie couldn't keep her hands off the guys, hugging them, laughing at everything they said. Dash was in his element, shining, though even tonight there was still something bittersweet about his smile. Hawke and Leo were happily draped with groupies. They were all the most content I'd ever seen them. Clearly this was what each of them was meant to do.

There was no sign of the usual bickering and harassment that I'd witnessed every day for the past week. They were like a tight-knit, albeit slightly dysfunctional, family. Even though they argued and pushed each other's buttons, their love for each other was undeniable. Tonight, their feelings were as clear as the full moon outside.

Seeing the group on stage, in sync, playing together, feeding off of each other, high on their own music—was hot as hell. They transformed into four sex gods and one hell of a rock goddess, dominating the stage, captivating the audience, making women of all ages moan and shed their panties.

Of course, many of the ladies were panting at the visuals, too—the way Dash ground his hips as if he was making love to his guitar, the raw rhythm and power of Synner's drumming, the deftness of Leo's fingers as they danced over the keyboard, the skill and speed with which Hawke played his bass, Indie's energy and sexy, expressive voice as she belted out the lyrics.

The show had been exhilarating—music thumping, the crowd pumping, technicolor lights dancing to the beat. Each song better than the last. Two of the best hours of my life, and I'd gotten to do it backstage, watching from the wings by Dare's side.

"Although," Leo now said, leaning forward to be heard, "we were a little off on—"

"Shut up and enjoy the glory, Leo," Hawke said. "It was fucking perfect tonight. *WE* were perfect."

Leo's face got hard. "It's Lynx, you fuckwad. My name is *Lynx*."

"Your name is Leo," Indie said, pointing at him. "And it's staying that way. We are not going to call you Lynx. Ever. Give it up already, while you've still got some dignity intact."

Leo looked ready to pout, but then the brunette on his right spoke.

"Leo?" she said, her voice as smooth and velvety as her brown skin. "That's kinda sexy." She purred as she petted his arm.

"Totally," said the blonde on his left. "Like a lion. You can be king of *my* jungle anytime." She took hold of his jaw, started to bring his mouth to hers, when Hawke put his hand between them.

"Sorry, babe, but there's already a queen of Leo's jungle." Hawke turned her face to him while Leo looked half-relieved, half-disappointed. Hawke's voice dipped into a low and sensual territory. "But, tonight, you can make *me* roar."

Indie's mouth fell open as she just shook her head. "You do realize that lions don't actually live in a *jungle*, right? Oh, fuck it. Never mind." Then she shrugged and went back to dazzling the cute guy sitting next to her with a brilliant smile.

I looked over at Synner to see if he'd noticed—he usually did—but he was too busy talking to Dalia.

Dax stared slack-jawed at the girls fawning over Leo and Hawke, drooling on the table. Without taking his eyes off of the women, he hit Dash's arm.

"Just this very minute I discovered I have musical talent. Can I join your band?"

Dash laughed, shaking his head, his arm draped around a stunning blonde.

"You don't have a musical bone in your body." Dalia turned away from Synner for a moment. "And a musical boner for groupies doesn't count."

"Okay, fine!" Dax laughed. "Then I can be your muscle. How about I go on tour with you as a roadie?" He flexed one well-toned bicep. "I play football, you know."

"How about you finish school first." Dare smacked the back of Dax's head, and Dax glared at him. If we weren't sitting in a restaurant, he probably would have pounced on Dare right then.

God, I loved it. Every single moment.

I hated to miss anything by going to the ladies' room, but guzzling water instead of downing shots tended to have an...*effect*.

When I came out of the stall, Dalia was freshening up her lip gloss. Our eyes met in the mirror as I washed my hands, and she beamed at me.

"So..." she said, "we haven't had a chance to talk yet, but it looks like things are good."

I nodded, unable to wipe the delirious smile from my face. "Really good," I said.

She tilted her head to one side. "You seem...different."

"I am," I said. "I'm trying to be."

"Dare said something about rehab?"

Oh, wow. He'd told his family, then. He was so close to Dalia and Dax, and since they'd unfortunately been privy to some of my past fuck-ups, I supposed it made sense to share the good news with them.

Regardless, I was a little thrown. It was hard to come to terms with the fact that a stint in rehab wasn't something to feel shame over. Shedding years of McKinley conditioning was easier said than done.

"Who'd have thought, right?" I smiled, trying to hide my discomfort. "Getting clean in Amsterdam of all places. Oh, the irony."

Dalia laughed, then reached over to squeeze my arm. "He's so proud of you, Ree," she said. "I don't know if you realize how huge this is to him. Our mom…" Her eyes started to water and she had to swallow a couple of times before she could continue. "She's never made it through." Her voice was tight. "She's tried so many times, but never stuck it out no matter how much we begged her. Dare has always felt like we weren't enough for her, like *he* wasn't enough. And now that you've made it through…" A couple of tears slipped out and she threw her arms around me, squeezing me tight. "You've made him feel like he is enough. Finally. He can't stop bragging about how brave you are, how strong, how amazing." She pulled back to look at me, her face wet, an immense grin getting in the way of the tears. "How much he loves you."

My own eyes began to sting as I hugged her to me again. "Thank you," I finally said.

See, Ree? Nothing to be ashamed of.

"No." Dalia pulled away and wiped at her eyes. "Thank YOU. Now I don't have to hunt you down and kick your ass." Her laughter sparkled around us, echoing off the restroom tiles.

We walked back out to the table arm in arm. She leaned down to say something to Synner as she slid into the seat next to him, and he laughed.

My eyes sought out Dare. He and Dash had stepped away from the group and were locked in an intense conversation by the bar. The closer I came, the clearer their words became.

"...you don't think they deserve to know?" Dare shook his head. "It just doesn't seem right to keep this from them."

"We don't know anything so let's not spoil the end of their trip. They'll be going back to reality soon enough." Dash noticed me nearing, and his voice dipped. "No need to scare them unnecessarily."

Dare's eyes met mine.

"Everything okay?" I asked.

"As far as we know, it is." Dare glanced at Dash, then back at me. "You okay? Is this too much tonight? Do you want to get going?"

He put his arm around me and started leading me away. I couldn't help but glance back at Dash, my curiosity spiked by the worried look on his face.

Something was going on that they weren't telling me about.

All I could think was that something was wrong with Dare's mom. Because why else would the two brothers be talking about spoiling Dalia and Dax's trip?

I opened my mouth to ask again, but then quickly shut it. They obviously didn't want me in on the issue. I was just going to have to wait until Dare was ready to talk.

I would be patient with him. Just like he had been patient with me.

After all, we had all the time in the world.

seventeen
Reagan

"Hey, not near the food!" Dax groaned the next morning as he sat down at the table.

Dare broke our kiss, flipped the finished pancakes onto a plate, then poured more batter into the hot skillet. Grinning at Dax over his shoulder, he pulled me toward him again and kissed me so hard my toes curled in my flip-flops.

"God, Dare," Dax said. "Get a room."

Without releasing my lips, Dare yanked the dishtowel hanging off the front of the oven and threw it at Dax.

"Leave 'em alone," Dash said, smacking the back of Dax's head, whose eyes narrowed dangerously as he sized up his older brother.

"Watch it, old man," Dax said. "I'm not afraid to take you down a few notches. And I'm not going to go easy on you just because you're famous."

"WHO," Dash laughed and hit his head again,

"are you calling OLD?"

For a brief second Dax stared at him, then he was up, flying across the table, and tackling Dash to the ground. They wrestled around, knocking over chairs, banging into cabinets, making enough noise to wake anybody who may have been still sleeping.

Dash laughed even as Dax pinned him to the ground.

"Okay, okay," Dash said. "I give up."

"Pansy." Dare shook his head. "I can't believe we're actually related. You NEVER give up. Especially not to Dax."

"*Uncle*," Dax said, not letting Dash up. "You've got to say *uncle*."

"Fine. UNCLE." Dash grinned, and I could feel Dare smile behind me. "So this is what it's like to have brothers."

"That's *right*." Dax got up, a smug look on his face. "And THIS is what it's like to get smacked down by your brother."

"Dax would know," Dare said. "He's had a LOT of experience with that."

Dax pointed at Dare. "I can take you next." Then he looked around, his brow furrowing. "Speaking of getting smacked down, where the hell is Dalia?"

Dash sat up. "She's not on the couch?"

Dax shook his head. "She wasn't there when I got up."

"She must be in the sh—" Dash started to say, but stopped when Synner's door swung open.

Synner backed out of his room, his lips firmly glued to Dalia's.

There was a moment of stunned silence in the room as we all stared. Dalia wound her arms around Synner's neck as he slid his hands down the small of her back, over the swell of her ass and squarely took hold.

Synner actually SQUEEZED Dalia's butt. In front of her three brothers.

Time truly felt like it stopped.

Then all hell broke loose.

Dash leapt to his feet while Dare lunged for Dax, who struggled to get free of Dare's steely hold, a murderous expression on his face.

Dash tapped Synner on the shoulder, and as he turned his head, Dash punched him in the face. Synner reeled from the hit, a line of curses flying out of his mouth.

"Bloody hell, Dash! You just broke my fucking nose." He was blinking his eyes, his hands pressed against the bridge of his nose. When he pulled them away, they were smeared with blood. "What the fuck is your problem? I'm your fucking bandmate."

"And she's my fucking SISTER!" Dash grabbed hold of Dalia's wrist and yanked her behind him.

"DASH!" Dalia tugged her arm free. "STOP IT!

I'm a grown woman."

"She is, indeed." Synner grinned even as the blood seeped out of his nose. "Best piece of tail—"

Dax roared and Dare swung him around, shoving him into the kitchen and sending him sputtering to the floor at my feet. Then he launched himself at Synner, hitting him square in the jaw.

"LITTLE sister," Dare roared, his chest heaving. "She's our little sister, you prick!"

Dax had gotten up and was now also charging at Synner, but Dalia dove for his feet, tackling him to the ground. Then she scrambled up onto his chest and caught him in a choke-hold.

"Cut. It. Out." She got right in Dax's face. "NOW, Dax!" Then she looked up at Dare and Dash. "Every single testosterone-filled Wilde better back the fuck off. If you hit him again, I will knock the shit out of all three of you." She punched Dax's shoulder as he started to struggle under her. "I'm not kidding, Dax. I am nineteen years old. You guys don't get to pull this shit anymore. I will sleep with whoever I want, whenever the fuck I want." She leaned into Dax, causing him to grunt in pain. "Am I making myself clear?!"

Dax glared at Synner, but he nodded reluctantly.

Dalia rose to her feet and placed herself in front of Synner, facing Dare and Dash. "How about you two asshats?" She poked each of them in the chest. Hard. "Have *you* got it?"

Neither of them took their eyes off Synner, but they nodded in unison.

"Good." She turned her back on them and reached up to gently touch Synner's face.

"Marry me, love," he said, gazing down at her in awe.

Dalia laughed, the sound wild and free, and shook her head. "Not a chance in hell."

A week later, Dalia and Dax were on their way home and my job in Paris was looming. Dare was putting the finishing touches on my phoenix on our last Sunday together.

Strangely, I'd come to love the sound of the tattoo gun humming, and no longer minded the sting of the needles so much. What I loved most, though, was watching Dare work. The more complete my bird became, the closer I felt to him. Having his creation on my skin made me feel like I had a part of him etched into *me*.

The buzzing stopped, and Dare wiped off my skin, taking a moment to gaze at his work.

"It's done," he said quietly. "You look...beautiful."

"I need to see it." I couldn't keep the smile from my face. "Before you cover it up."

He pulled me up and guided me over to the

mirror, never letting go of my hand.

The lines of the tattoo swooped and swirled down my right side, the bird's tail feathers curling at my hip. Its wings gracefully brushed my ribs, spread as if in flight, rising above the remains of the phoenix's rebirth. Fire licked the edges of the feathers, making them appear as if they were bursting into flames of red and gold.

It was incredible.

My beautiful bird made me feel whole in a way I never had before. It made me feel new, reborn as the person I was truly meant to be. As Ree.

Reagan was gone, the last vestiges of her had been colored over, released into the flames of this phoenix. The lines of my life had been redrawn, redefined, and filled in.

I'd come home at last.

I just wished I didn't have to leave tomorrow. The only thing that made the looming separation less painful was the reminder that Dare would be joining me in two weeks. We'd made it through longer and rougher periods before. We'd survive the distance once again. With ease, this time.

Especially considering that things were different. Now that I was branded by his own hands, I felt more like I belonged to him than I ever had before. Dare owned me—mind, body, and soul. And he always would from this day forth. Even if I didn't know all the things the future held for us, that much I knew was true.

"What do you think?" he asked, closing the space between us with one step, melding my back against his front.

"It's…perfect."

Our eyes met in the mirror, burning with need for each other.

A devious grin spread across his lips. "Almost," he said, reaching for the hem of my tank.

The shirt slid over my head, and he tossed it into a nearby chair. Then he tugged my skirt over my hips, letting it drop to the floor, leaving me standing in front of him in only my bra and panties. Dare's eyes were glued to my reflection as one of his hands slid around my side to skim my stomach while the other glided down to my ass, cupping and palming me.

"Already wet." He practically growled the words. "And so ready for me."

"I'm always ready for you." I swallowed, my body tingling all over, a deep ache between my legs calling for Dare's touch.

He unclasped my bra and slid the silky fabric off my arms, then his hands came up on either side to caress the tender flesh of my breasts. I leaned back against him, watching in the mirror as he teased my nipples into tight, tingling buds, feeling my panties get wetter and wetter with each pass of his fingers.

I moaned, turning my head, and his lips found mine, hungry and urgent. God, he was ravenous, always so deliciously wanting more. A thrill ran through me as his tongue met mine and they tangled together, tasting each other. His fingers left my breasts to thread through my hair as he held my head captive and devoured my lips.

Then he was kissing my jaw, making his way to my ear. Shivers flowed through me as he sucked the lobe into his mouth, nibbling at it with his teeth, sending jolts of electricity to my core. He kissed down my neck to my shoulder, his breath hot, his tongue fiery, his need insatiable.

As was mine.

I ached to feel all of him, to own him as he owned me.

And tonight I would.

Every movement and every flick of his tongue had that spot between my thighs throbbing harder and harder. His hands skimmed back down my body, grazing my nipples for just a moment, making them tighten in pleasure before he headed lower. I gasped when his fingers settled on the edge of my panties, pulsing with even greater intensity as I imagined them finally discovering my swollen clit.

A smile lifted his lips. "Sapphire?" he said, staring at my last remaining bit of clothing. "I haven't seen these before."

"You like?" I shimmied my hips a little.

"I like. I especially like how easily they come off."

His hands slipped under the light fabric and he slid my underwear down with deliberate leisure over my hips, guiding them all the way to the floor, inch by inch, driving me wild with want, setting my entire body aflame.

He looked up at me, feral and hungry. "Now you're perfect," he said, his hands slowly roaming over my naked skin. "Wearing only your phoenix and your smile."

Then he pushed my back against the bolted mirror and knelt before me, a dark, wicked look on his face as he slid his hand up one leg, lifted it, and placed it on his shoulder, completely opening me up to him. The ache between my legs grew to a fevered pitch at the thrill of being so fully bared. His fingers trailed along my inner thigh, getting closer and closer until he was circling my folds, almost grazing my core.

"Dare." I moaned, leaning back against the cool, sleek surface, my heart beating a wild rhythm of primal desire. The ache inside me grew to be so vast I was sure just one touch would send me over the edge. "Please."

"Please what?" He pressed my thighs open farther and I pushed my hips toward him, feeling his sharp exhale bathing my clit in warmth. *So close.* He was so fucking close to it. I needed him to take me into his mouth and—

"Lick me." I panted the words, the feel of his hot breath teasing me, taunting me to new heights, the knowledge that his tongue had to be just millimeters away almost killing me. "Please, Dare. I need you."

His tongue flicked out, and I moaned loudly, thrusting my hips forward, begging, needing. When it came again more slowly, I cried out his name.

"*Mmmm*...sweeter than ever." He groaned into my heat, his face grinding against my pelvis. "I love how you taste, Ree. I could do this all fucking day long."

"I'd let you." I gasped out the words just as his lips wrapped around my clit and he sucked me into his mouth, simultaneously lifting my other leg over his other shoulder, completely putting me at his mercy.

Explosions of fireworks burst in my core, radiating from where his mouth heated me to the rest of my body. The rhythm of his tongue moving against me and delving into me rocked me higher and higher until I was shaking with pent up pleasure, Dare's name a cry buried deep in my chest, clamoring for release.

"Do it, baby," he said as if he'd read my need. "Say it. Scream it. Let go."

His words sent me over the edge, screaming out his name as I rode tidal waves of pleasure.

When the spasms slowed, I realized he was still on his knees, gazing at me from below, watching the ecstasy of my orgasm subside, the most amazing look of wonder on his face. He slipped my legs off his shoulders, and slowly kissed his way up my body, forcing me deeper against the mirror as he covered my mouth with his.

"My turn," I purred into his kiss, imprinting my naughty grin into his lips as I switched our positions so his back was to the mirror now. "I want to taste you. All of you."

Grasping the hem of his white t-shirt, I lifted it up and over his head. God, he was so fucking beautiful. I let my hands roam over the contours of his chest and stomach, relishing the feel of his smooth, tight skin. He watched me admire him, a loving smile lighting his face.

As my hands dipped lower, his breathing hitched and his abs tightened. I loved that I turned him on as much as he did me. I gripped the front of his jeans and pulled, ripping open the button fly, freeing him in a single tug. He was gloriously commando, and as his pants slid down to his feet, I took the length of him into my hands.

He groaned at the feel of my hands sliding up and down his velvety hardness, but when I got on my knees in front of him and opened my lips around him, he threaded his fingers through my hair and shook his head.

"Ree," he said, his voice wavering a little. "I don't know how long I can—oh, *fuck*."

I opened my mouth and swirled my tongue around the tip of him and he sucked in a sharp breath. Teasing my way along his shaft, I ran my fingers up and down his inner thighs, the sounds of explicit pleasure spilling from his mouth turning me on even more.

Parting my lips wider, I took in as much of his thick length as I could, pulling him in as far as he would go, and worshiping him with my tongue. A low growl rumbled from deep down in his chest, and his knees buckled slightly.

"Jesus, Ree," he said, each word a strained groan. "I'm at your mercy."

So I did it again.

And again.

And again.

Each time, I took him deeper, pushing past thresholds, owning him with my mouth.

"*Reeee…*" My name was a plea on his lips as his hips rocked to the pace I set. Wrapping one hand around him, I continued to move back and forth, increasing the speed and intensity. "*Fuck*, Ree."

His head fell back, hitting the glass behind him as he began moaning my name over and over again, spasms ripping through him, his own pleasure utterly out of his control. Once the tremors finally ceased, he lifted me up and pressed his lips to mine, kissing me so deeply I could feel it vibrate to the depth of my soul.

"I fucking love you. You know that, right?" he said against my lips.

"You are mine," I whispered back. "Mine to love, mine to have, mine to own."

He nodded. "And you, my beautiful Ree, are mine. All mine. Now and always."

eighteen
Dare

Perched on the edge on my bed, I watched Ree bend over to tighten the clasps on her sandals. I was surrounded by her sweet scent and an even more delicious view. My cock stirred. Apparently last night's double performance and this morning's encore wasn't enough. When it came to Ree, nothing was ever enough.

Goddamn it. I was going to go insane over the next two weeks.

As if sensing my eyes trail down her body, she looked at me over her shoulder and shot me a dazzling smile. "Stop staring at my ass like you want a bite," she said with a laugh. "I'm going to miss my plane."

"I'll buy you another ticket." I walked over and stood behind her, running my fingers through her hair then slowly trailing them down her spine, vertebra by vertebra, making her breath quicken into raspy, little pants.

"Dare!" She shot up when my hand went lower. "Neither of us have money to waste."

"Would it really be a *waste?*" Gently palming her ass, I dipped my hand under her skirt to the lace-covered spot between her legs. "Your soaked panties tell a different story."

"*Fuck...*" She shut her eyes and relaxed against my chest, moaning as I slipped under the fabric and glided my fingers to the spot I knew would have her head spinning within seconds. My other hand soared up her stomach to cup her breast as my mouth latched onto her collarbone.

"I'm just trying to fill myself up on every part of you so that I don't completely lose my mind while we're apart," I said as I kissed my way up her neck to her earlobe. I took the sensitive flesh between my teeth and sucked as I thrust a finger inside her, causing her to cry out and push her hips deeper into me.

"There's...always...phone...sex..." Her breathing grew more erratic, her words coming out in rapid spurts matching the pace of my hand. "I can call...describe the silky thong I'm wearing...tell you how I'm touching myself and wishing it was you doing it...how hot and wet you make me...how badly I need to have you inside me..."

"Fuck. Keep talking like that and I might never let you leave."

I was only half-kidding.

There was a loud pound on my bedroom door and we both jumped. "HURRY UP! You're going to be late for the airport!"

Indie. *Of course.*

"Looks like it's time to go, baby," I said into her ear, my fingers thrusting deeper, my thumb massaging faster. "So come for me."

"REE!" *Bang.* "DARE!" *Pound.* "COME!" *Bang.* ON!" *Pound.*

"COMING!" Ree cried out. "Oh, god…coming!"

And she did. She collapsed into my arms with the sweetest moan and my name on her lips.

Just the way I liked.

"Oh, god." She spun around and fumbled with her skirt, her cheeks a deep crimson that offset the watery hues of her eyes. "Is that the send-off you give all your girlfriends?"

"Only the special ones," I said. "I'm just making sure that you don't forget my talented hands when you're surrounded by all those painters back in Paris. You know how an artist can be."

"Yeah, an egotistical pain in the ass."

"Interesting." I shot her a wicked grin. "I was going to say a skilled *pleasure* in the—"

"You're impossible, Wilde." She rolled her eyes and pecked me on the lips, her bubbly laughter rousing a warmth inside me that no one else ever had.

The girl had no idea how beautiful she was. And, most of the time, she was adorably unaware of her full effect on me. Not just my body, but my heart.

Jesus. I was starting to sound like a freaking chick.

At least I wasn't spouting this shit out loud. Though she was amazing...and leaving momentarily.

Oh, what the hell.

"I'm going to miss you," I told her. "I'm going to miss your smart mouth, and especially this smile." I traced her bottom lip with my thumb. "I fucking love your smile, Ree."

"You'll call, right?" She narrowed her eyes at me. "Every day, even though you *hate* phones with a passion?"

"Well, now that you promised to talk dirty to me, I'm calling you before your plane even gets in the air." The truth was that ever since Ree had gone to rehab, I didn't mind the phone thing as much. It had kept us close, but I'd also learned more about her. She'd opened up on those calls in ways she hadn't before. "Although, video calls have the added benefit of visuals—"

"Dare!" She giggled and smacked my arm, but then quickly sobered. "Thank you."

"For what?" I arched an eyebrow, the sudden gravity of her tone surprising me.

"For supporting me," she said. "For pushing me to get help and fight for the future even when I didn't think it was possible."

"With you and me together…anything is possible."

My lips met hers in a soft, deep kiss.

Fuck. I didn't want to let her go.

"Two parts?" she breathed when we pulled apart.

"No. Not today." I shook my head and claimed her mouth again. "Today, we're just one whole, Ree."

Ree was checking her luggage when my phone vibrated.

"Mom? Can I call you—"

"Daren!" Her voice was panicked, desperate. "Rex is hurt. He come…he came and he…Daren…he—"

"Mom, slow down. Take a deep breath. What happened to Rex?"

"He. Found. Me," she said between gasps.

"Rex did?" She wasn't making any sense.

"Your FATHER."

I turned away from the counter where Ree still stood, and walked toward the front windows. "*What?!*"

"He's out, Daren."

My blood turned to ice. "Of Rykers?"

"He's here," she said. "In the city."

"But you're in L.A. You're still in L.A., right? How the hell did he find you?"

"I don't know. He told Rex to thank someone called The Mayor for the beating. He hurt him bad, Daren." She started sobbing. "He broke Rex's arm and gave him a concussion."

"Did you just say *the mayor?*" The ice in my veins cracked, splintered, cut through me.

"One of his many thugs, I'm sure." She sniffled. "I was at work when he came to the house, thank god." She was silent for a moment, then said in a small voice, "I don't know if I'm strong enough to fight him. The police aren't very helpful. They have no evidence aside from Rex's ID and Daren's past record. They put a warrant out, but you know how good your father is at evading arrest."

"Go to the hospital and stay with Rex," I said. "You'll be safe there. I'm getting on the next flight."

"NO!" She sounded panicked, and I could almost imagine her big, hazel eyes widening. "He'll kill…I…I don't know what he'll do if he sees you again. You can't come here. It's not safe for you."

"It's not safe for you either, Mom. I'm not leaving you alone with that bastard."

"No, Daren—"

"STOP calling me that! That's *his* name!" Not mine. *Never* mine.

"*Dare…*"

"I'm coming," I said. "Go to Rex. I'll be there tonight." Then I hung up.

"Is everything okay?" Ree walked up to me, ticket in hand, her eyes raking over my face. "You look like you've just seen a ghost."

More like a fucking demon. I shook my head and cleared my throat. "Everything is fine. Perfect."

I squeezed her tightly to me, avoiding her eyes. Lying to Ree killed me, but how could I tell her? She'd never leave. She'd demand to go back to the States with me, and I couldn't put her life in danger. I loved her too much for that.

It was bad enough that Dax and Dalia were home already, and my dad might find them, too. FUCK. I had to get on a plane. NOW.

I pulled Ree closer, breathing her in, memorizing her scent, the feel of her even as I was sending up a silent thanks for the timing of this job. She would be happy and busy, following her dream, while I dealt with my nightmare.

Then I'd fly back to Paris to be with her just as we planned.

I pressed my lips to her forehead. "See you in two weeks."

She stood on her tiptoes and wrapped her hands around my neck. "Don't you dare be late."

"I wouldn't dream of it, Princess." My chest clenched as our lips met.

Then Ree was walking away from me, biting her lip to keep from crying. I waited until she was out of sight before sprinting to the nearest airline counter and booking a seat on the next flight to Los Angeles.

My mind raced with all the things I needed to do even as I was dialing Dash's number. A cold, hard determination settled over me. I would deal with my father. And, god-willing, I'd implicate the fucking mayor if I could for putting my family and Rex's life in danger.

And, then I'd make him pay for everything he'd done to Ree.

I only hoped I could do it all in two weeks.

Without casualties.

nineteen
Reagan

Two weeks.

What had felt like a lifetime when we'd said goodbye in Amsterdam had actually flown by in the blink of an eye. Preparing for La Période Bleue's international show was unbelievably time-consuming, especially since we were working with several other galleries across the city. I was often up until the early hours of the morning, tackling the mountain of paperwork and scheduling that needed to be coordinated to pull this off. My days were spent schmoozing gallery owners and meeting artists from all around the world.

To put it lightly, I was *extremely* busy.

But I was back in the city of love and light, feeling more at home than I ever had anywhere else, and anxiously awaiting Dare's arrival so real life could finally start.

It was an exquisite torture to be living in his

apartment—surrounded by his art, his scent, his brushes. I slept between his sheets, wore his t-shirt to bed, lived and breathed him, while the only direct contact I actually had was his voice in my ear. We spoke almost every night—and if we failed to connect for some reason, I always woke up to a message from him by dawn's light.

I was missing him like crazy, and today—FINALLY—he would, once again, be mine.

Last night, my call had gone straight to his voicemail. And there hadn't been a message from him this morning, which was a little odd. However, considering his plane was getting in this afternoon, it didn't really matter. I was going to get my hands on him in mere hours. My body was already humming in anticipation of seeing him, touching him, feeling his presence fill me again.

I'd spent the morning getting ready—my hair hung down my back just the way he liked it, and I'd picked out my favorite dress. But that was all I wore—I was going commando just for him.

I couldn't keep the ecstatic smile from my face.

Nothing was going to spoil my happiness today.

And it was *happiness*. Deep, intense, pure joy. I'd never felt this good in my entire life. I knew that some people spent their lives bathed in the kind of joy that seeped into their bones and infused everything they did, every choice they made, how they viewed the world.

But that had never been my life. Until now.

The airport was busy, and I hurried to the arrival gate, scanning the crowd as I walked. I hadn't checked to see if his flight was on time, I'd just rushed over, unable to wait for him any longer.

People streamed through the airport, most of them clearly having just gotten off a plane, bags slung over their shoulders, stretching their bodies from being cramped up. And when they cleared out, when no more people were walking from the arrival gate, I started to get concerned.

He'd bought his ticket the day before I'd left, and I knew his flight should have arrived a little before two. But it was now almost three. I walked over to a monitor to check the arrival and departure listings. His plane had arrived on time.

But, still, no Dare.

My heart started thumping, my mind racing, trying to figure out why he wouldn't have been on the plane. I checked my messages to see if I'd missed one. Maybe he'd texted me or left a voicemail about a change in his flight plans.

Maybe something had happened in Amsterdam.

Maybe he didn't want me anymore.

NO. No, I knew that couldn't be true. And I was not going to allow negative thoughts to ruin this moment.

I dialed his number but, once again, it went straight to voicemail. Then I sent him a quick text and drummed my fingers against my phone as I waited for his reply.

Nothing.

I tried Dash's number, but he didn't pick up either, so I left a message, then dialed Dalia. And even Dax.

Fucking hell. Why wasn't anyone answering their fucking phone?

Trying not to panic, I headed over to the baggage claim area to see if maybe I'd somehow missed him.

The carousel was deserted when I got there.

Oh, god. I was rooted in place, unsure of what to do, who to call next, how I could reach him to find out what was going on.

In that exact moment, my phone buzzed.

I glanced at the screen.

Dalia.

Relief flooded my body. She must have gotten my message. She would—

"Ree?" Dalia said, her voice tight with tears. "You've got to come. Dare's—" She broke off, sobbing into the phone.

"*What?*" She was crying too hard to speak, but panic had overtaken me at the sound in her voice.

I needed her to tell me NOW. "*Dare's WHAT?*"

"He's been hurt. Oh god, Ree. He's in intensive care. They don't know if he'll—"

Chills shuddered through me, my whole body went numb. I started shaking my head. This couldn't...HE couldn't...

"Where is he, Dalia? *Where?!*"

"New York," she said. "And, Ree? Hurry. *Please.* They don't..." Her voice quivered as she choked on the words. "...they don't know if he'll make it."

Reagan and Dare's story continues in...

untamed

episode 4: wild at heart

Untamed 4: Wild at Heart

With his dad hell-bent on destroying him, Dare's life hangs in the balance. Fearing the worst, Reagan rushes from Paris to New York, hoping to get to him in time, only to find their entire world collapsing around them.

The threat is too real, risk too high, death too possible. Unfair doesn't even begin to cover it.

Two wild hearts that belong together, trapped in a world trying to break them apart. But a love this strong has to survive...doesn't it?

AVAILABLE NOW
All books in the series now available

Want to be emailed when Victoria and Jen release a new book?

Get on the Mailing List!

Enter your email address at either Victoria's site (victoriagreenauthor.blogspot.ca) or Jen's site (www.jmeyersbooks.com/the-list), and you'll be the first to hear when new books are available. Your address will never be shared and you'll only get emailed when a book has been released or is newly available.

acknowledgements

Our biggest thanks, as always, goes to our editor, Stevan Knapp. He's a marvel with a red pen, and makes our books all shiny and pretty.

So many thanks to Justin, Jena, Julie, and Helen for the amazing support they have given us. We can't tell you how much we appreciate it. And to Christy Lynn for being our tattoo expert and answering all of our questions—Dare definitely owes you a tattoo.

Many, many thanks to our early readers and reviewers for being so willing to post your reviews quickly and in many places. That's such a huge help to us! And to all the bloggers and readers who have become so excited about this series, taking Reagan and Dare into your hearts, and helping us spread the word—your support and enthusiasm is incredible, and we cannot thank you enough. We love you guys!

And lastly, we thank *you* for reading our books. You're the reason we write.

about the authors

Victoria Green has a soft spot for unspoken love and second chances. A travel junkie at heart, she believes in true love, good chocolate, great films, and swoon-worthy books. She lives in Canada with her high school sweetheart (who's graduated to fiancé) and their pack of slightly crazy, but lovable puppies.

She is also the author of *Silver Heart*. When she's not writing hot and steamy romances, she writes Young Adult adventures under a different name.

Visit her online at victoriagreenauthor.blogspot.ca.

Jen Meyers grew up in Vermont, spent three years in Germany when she was a kid, and now lives in central New York. When she's not reading or writing, she's chasing after her four kids, playing outside, relishing the few quiet moments she gets with her husband, and forgetting to make dinner.

She is the author of the highly-rated Intangible series, a young adult contemporary fantasy, and numerous contemporary romance novels.

Visit Jen online at www.jmeyersbooks.com.

Made in the USA
Columbia, SC
21 October 2021